THE **FORTUNES** OF **TEXAS**

SHIPMENT 1

Healing Dr. Fortune by Judy Duarte
Mendoza's Return by Susan Crosby
Fortune's Just Desserts by Marie Ferrarella
Fortune's Secret Baby by Christyne Butler
Fortune Found by Victoria Pade
Fortune's Cinderella by Karen Templeton

SHIPMENT 2

Fortune's Valentine Bride by Marie Ferrarella
Mendoza's Miracle by Judy Duarte
Fortune's Hero by Susan Crosby
Fortune's Unexpected Groom by Nancy Robards Thompson
Fortune's Perfect Match by Allison Leigh
Her New Year's Fortune by Allison Leigh

SHIPMENT 3

A Date with Fortune by Susan Crosby
A Small Fortune by Marie Ferrarella
Marry Me, Mendoza! by Judy Duarte
Expecting Fortune's Heir by Cindy Kirk
A Change of Fortune by Crystal Green
Happy New Year, Baby Fortune! by Leanne Banks
A Sweetheart for Jude Fortune by Cindy Kirk

SHIPMENT 4

Lassoed by Fortune by Marie Ferrarella
A House Full of Fortunes! by Judy Duarte
Falling for Fortune by Nancy Robards Thompson
Fortune's Prince by Allison Leigh
A Royal Fortune by Judy Duarte
Fortune's Little Heartbreaker by Cindy Kirk

SHIPMENT 5

Mendoza's Secret Fortune by Marie Ferrarella
The Taming of Delaney Fortune by Michelle Major
My Fair Fortune by Nancy Robards Thompson
Fortune's June Bride by Allison Leigh
Plain Jane and the Playboy by Marie Ferrarella
Valentine's Fortune by Allison Leigh

SHIPMENT 6

Triple Trouble by Lois Faye Dyer
Fortune's Woman by RaeAnne Thayne
A Fortune Wedding by Kristin Hardy
Her Good Fortune by Marie Ferrarella
A Tycoon in Texas by Crystal Green
In a Texas Minute by Stella Bagwell

SHIPMENT 7

Cowboy at Midnight by Ann Major
A Baby Changes Everything by Marie Ferrarella
In the Arms of the Law by Peggy Moreland
Lone Star Rancher by Laurie Paige
The Good Doctor by Karen Rose Smith
The Debutante by Elizabeth Bevarly

SHIPMENT 8

Keeping Her Safe by Myrna Mackenzie
The Law of Attraction by Kristi Gold
Once a Rebel by Sheri WhiteFeather
Military Man by Marie Ferrarella
Fortune's Legacy by Maureen Child
The Reckoning by Christie Ridgway

THE **FORTUNES** OF **TEXAS**

FORTUNE'S VALENTINE BRIDE

―――――― ✿ ――――――

USA TODAY BESTSELLING AUTHOR

Marie Ferrarella

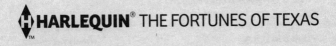

HARLEQUIN® THE FORTUNES OF TEXAS

Special thanks and acknowledgment are given to Marie Ferrarella for her contribution to the Fortunes of Texas: Whirlwind Romance continuity.

Recycling programs for this product may not exist in your area.

ISBN-13: 978-1-335-68040-2

Fortune's Valentine Bride

Printed in U.S.A.

HARLEQUIN®
www.Harlequin.com

USA TODAY bestselling and RITA® Award–winning author **Marie Ferrarella** has written more than two hundred and fifty books for Harlequin, some under the name Marie Nicole. Her romances are beloved by fans worldwide. Visit her website, marieferrarella.com.

To
Helen with love,
despite the fact
that she has now moved
to a galaxy far, far
away.

Chapter 1

"Don't take this the wrong way, Blake," Wendy Mendoza said to her brother as she tried, and failed, to find a comfortable spot on her bed, "but with all this hovering about you're doing, I'm beginning to feel like a watched pot."

Blake Fortune dragged over the chair he'd brought into his younger sister's bedroom earlier and straddled it. "Isn't that actually a good thing?" he pointed out. "Watched pots aren't supposed to boil, or, in your case, give birth prematurely."

Which was, between the terbutaline injections to stop her contractions and the enforced bed rest, exactly what the doctor and she were trying to prevent.

But that didn't mean that she had to be happy about this state of affairs, Blake knew. And the longer she lay there, inert, the more restless she grew.

"Isn't there something you could be doing?" she pressed, more accustomed to his teasing than his concern. "I mean, I really do appreciate you deciding to drop everything and come running back to Red Rock to hold my hand, but having everyone practically walking on eggshells around me is *really* making me feel very tense and nervous."

Which was, he knew, counterproductive to what they were all really trying to do—keep her pregnant until the baby was strong enough to survive on its own when she emerged.

"If this keeps up," Wendy warned, "I'm going to wind up giving birth to a neurotic baby who's going to go straight from the delivery room to some psychiatrist's couch."

Blake laughed, shaking his head. At least she hadn't lost her offbeat sense of humor. The whole family had gone through one hell of a trauma when that tornado had hit. And then on top of that, when Wendy had suddenly gone into premature labor, it had put a scare into all of them.

Thank God for modern medicine, he thought. Now she was back to her feisty self—

except for not being able to get out of bed, he amended.

"Well, obviously the tornado had no effect on your imagination," he commented. But one look at her expression told him that she was being serious. She wanted him out of her bedroom. He supposed that if he were in her place, he might feel a bit crowded, too. "You've already kicked me out of your house to bunk with Scott at his place," he reminded her. "You want me to go altogether?"

Reaching out, Wendy caught her brother's hand and threaded her fingers through his. She loved all her siblings, but, as the baby of the family, Blake was the brother she was closest to. He was the second youngest. Together they were the bottom of the totem pole.

"No, I don't want you to go altogether," she told him with feeling, "but I don't want you putting your life on hold because of me, either." He'd been her constant companion for two days now. It was time he got back to his career, to his life. "With computers and tele-conferencing, you could work anywhere. Why don't you set up a temporary office at Scott's and take care of business before Dad comes, breathing down your neck for dropping the ball, or whatever cliché he favors these days."

John Michael Fortune, who she felt certain

did love his family in his own, private way, was ultimately responsible for the turn her life had taken. If her father hadn't insisted on sending her here, to Red Rock, Texas, in hopes of waking up her heretofore sleeping work ethic, she might have never discovered the two ultimate passions of her life: baking and Marcos—not necessarily in that order.

Her newfound passion for baking and creating desserts had come to light when she had gone to work at the restaurant that Marcos managed for his aunt and uncle, who were friends of her parents. At the time it was clear that Marcos felt he was being saddled with her and that he thought she was a spoiled little rich girl, totally incapable of doing anything right.

Marcos had been looking to fire her, while she in turn was looking for ways to prove herself. What neither one had been looking for was a life commitment, but they'd found it, in spades. Now she was married to Marcos and expecting his child any day.

A baby that had almost been born nearly a month ago, thanks to the tornado that had ripped through Red Rock just minutes before her family, who had flown out for her Christmas Eve wedding, were to take off for Atlanta.

It still left her breathless when she thought about it. One minute, she was saying her goodbyes, the next, they were being all but buried alive in debris as the tornado buzz sawed through the airport, collapsing it all around them.

The shock of it all, including having Marcos's badly injured brother, Javier, lapse into a coma, was too much for her. She found herself going into labor *way* before she was anywhere near her due date. Luckily, her doctor was able to temporarily curtail her contractions with injections. The hope was that she could hold on long enough for the baby's lungs to develop sufficiently to sustain the infant outside the womb.

Right now the process seemed as if it was taking forever. And having Blake constantly slanting wary glances in her direction really wasn't helping anything, especially not her frame of mind.

The problem was Blake could see her side of it. If the tables were turned, he wouldn't want people hovering around him, either, no matter how much he loved them. "I suppose you have a point."

Wendy smiled broadly, relieved that Blake wasn't offended by her strongly worded "suggestion." But then, this was Blake and, most of the time, they really did think alike.

"Of course I do."

Blake was already focusing on another project, one that had gone begging for his attention much too long. It was time to stop allowing it to take a backseat and get started on it in earnest.

"Actually, there has been something I've been meaning to do ever since we were practically buried alive in that airport," he confessed to her.

Wendy wasn't sure she was following him. "You were thinking of business at a time like that?" she asked incredulously. "God, Blake, you're more like Dad than I thought."

No, he highly doubted that any one of his father's offspring would ever be placed in the same category as their dad. The man ate and slept business and, while he expected the same of his children, none of them, Blake thought, would ever measure up to the old man's expectations. Blake sincerely doubted that anyone—besides a robot—could.

"Not business exactly," he explained. For the moment, he moved his chair in even closer to Wendy's bed, lowering his voice. This was something he wasn't ready to share with the immediate world—at least not yet. "When it looked like we actually might not make it, I promised myself that if we *did* survive, I'd stop putting my life on hold and do what I should have done years ago."

Intrigued, Wendy sat up a little straighter in her bed. She pushed another one of the pillows behind her, tucking it against her back. "Go on," she encouraged, curious where this was going.

"I promised myself that, if I survived, I was going to go after the woman who I allowed to slip away all those years ago." Smiling broadly at the plan that was, even now, evolving and taking on layers in his mind, Blake paused a second for dramatic effect, then shared the woman's name. "Brittany Everett."

"I changed my mind," Wendy told him. "*Don't* go on." She blew out a breath, sincerely disappointed with Blake's revelation. She'd hoped that the socialite Brittany Everett, would be a thing of the past in Blake's life. Actually, she'd secretly been hoping that when her brother's thoughts finally took a more serious turn toward things of a romantic nature, it would be images of Katie Wallace that ramped up his body temperature.

Everyone but Blake, apparently, knew that Brittany was just a spoiled Daddy's girl. In addition, she was someone who gave all "Southern belles" a bad name.

Trying her best not to look annoyed, Wendy slumped back on her pillows.

"What do you *see* in that woman?" she demanded in frustration. Before Blake could answer, she held up her hand. She was in no mood to hear any accolades for a woman she had never liked. "I mean, other than the obvious—that she could tip over if she turned around too fast." The woman under discussion had a pretty face, a large chest—and a completely empty head, not to mention no heart to speak of.

Wendy was pregnant and her hormones were undoubtedly all over the charts, Blake reasoned, so he let her last comment go and only said defensively, "You don't know Brittany."

Now, there he was wrong, Wendy thought. "Oh, but I do, Blake, I really do," she countered. Fixing him with an exasperated look, she insisted, "Blake, she's not good enough for you."

He laughed. When Wendy was very young, she'd been very possessive of him and jealous of any time he spent with anyone besides her. He supposed that there was still a tiny bit of that little girl left, even though she was now a married woman.

"You'd say that about anybody."

His protest made her think of Katie. Katie was extremely likable and had a great deal going for her. Katie's family lived practically next door to hers in Atlanta, and they had all grown up together. She was kind, pretty and smart—and not even the least bit self-serving.

Brittany, on the other hand, was convinced

that the world existed only for her own pleasure. Not only that, but it all revolved around her, as well.

Granted, Brittany and Blake had dated during his senior year, but from what Wendy had heard via the grapevine, she hadn't changed a bit.

"No," Wendy said firmly, "I wouldn't."

But Blake was convinced that he was right and that she was only acting like the overprotective little sister she'd once been. "Yeah, you would," he insisted. "But that's okay. My mind's made up. I'm going to launch a campaign—"

Were they still talking about the same thing? "A campaign?" Wendy questioned, looking at her brother uncertainly.

"Uh-huh. A business campaign." This was the very strategy he'd been missing, he told himself. He had to approach this goal of his by using his strengths and his skills if he hoped to ever win his "prize." "That's what I should have done in the first place, instead of just backing away," he told Wendy. The more he talked about it, the more convinced he became that this was the right approach. "If I'd gone after Brittany the way I usually go after a new client, I would have won her over a long time ago." He nodded at his sister's swollen belly. "And then little Mary Anne would have another doting aunt when she's born."

God forbid, Wendy thought, all but biting her tongue to keep from voicing her thoughts out loud.

"You know," Blake continued as his thoughts fell into place, "your idea about setting up an office in Scott's house isn't half bad. If I want to approach this problem professionally—"

Wendy fought the desire to tell her brother that she'd been too hasty and had made a mistake. That she really needed him to hang around here and help her stave off the boredom.

But then, if this really was Blake's mindset, she knew that he would continue talking about Brittany and how wonderful he thought she was. She also knew that she would come very close to strangling her beloved brother if he went on and on about Brittany and her so-called attributes. If nothing else, it would make her nauseous as hell.

Still, she had to find a way to at least *try* to throw a monkey wrench into this absurd "campaign" plan of his. Not that she actually thought that the heartless Brittany would wind up marrying her brother. She knew the woman well enough to know that Brittany was too accustomed to being fawned over by a host of men to ever give that up for just one man.

But if Blake went all out to win Brittany

over, he would eventually have his heart cut out and handed to him—and not on a silver platter. Wendy was determined to do whatever it took to spare her brother that ultimate pain and humiliation.

But there was only so much she could physically do right now.

Wendy frowned, staring down at the bed that imprisoned her. Giving her word that she wouldn't get out of bed was the only way she had managed to bargain her discharge from a San Antonio hospital room. Her doctor had fully intended for her to remain in the hospital until such time as her baby was physically developed enough to be born. Complete bed rest was the only compromise available.

Which meant that she was going to need an ally to act in her place. More specifically, she needed the one woman who just might be able to get her brother to give up this ridiculous notion of asking Brittany Everett to become Mrs. Blake Fortune.

"If you're setting up your office," Wendy said, cutting in, "you might as well send for Katie and have her come join you."

Caught off guard by the suggestion, Blake stared at her. "Katie?" he echoed.

"Wallace," Wendy prompted needlessly. Katie was as much a part of her brother's life as anyone in the family. More, probably. "You know, your marketing assistant. Cute girl, twenty-four, stands about five foot five, has pretty brown hair and soft brown eyes—"

Blake snorted. "I know who Katie is." And then, as he replayed his sister's initial words in his head, he nodded. His frown faded. "You know, sending for Katie's not a half-bad idea, either."

Yes!

"Of course it's not a half-bad idea," Wendy informed him serenely, then couldn't help adding, "It's a completely wonderful idea.

"She can help you with your *work,*" she underscored pointedly, praying she could divert her brother's focus away from the girl he was mooning about and get him back on his usual track. Blake really was a very hard worker and a real asset to FortuneSouth Enterprises. This nonsense about Brittany was hopefully just that—nonsense. "Katie has wonderful organizational skills," Wendy reminded him.

Besides, Wendy added silently, if her brother interacted with Katie, maybe he'd forget about this stupid vow to win over Miss all wrong for him. Or at least feel too stupid saying it out loud in Katie's presence, which meant he wouldn't be putting whatever half-baked plan he was hatching into play.

Though they had never talked about it out loud, Wendy was certain that Katie had feelings for Blake. Maybe even loved him. It was all there, in her eyes.

Not that Blake ever looked, she thought, slanting a disparaging glance in his direction, which he seemed to miss totally.

"I'll get right on it," Blake was saying cheerfully. Rising from the chair, he stopped to brush a kiss against her cheek. "You're the best," he told Wendy with enthusiasm.

"Of course I am," she agreed, as he headed for the doorway.

"Katie, I need you."

Katie Wallace nearly dropped the receiver as Blake Fortune's voice echoed in her ear, uttering the words she had waited to hear for what felt like her entire life. Words that she'd been fairly convinced she was *never* going to hear.

Katie, I need you. He'd said it. Blake had actually said it.

To her.

They weren't in the middle of an incredibly long meeting, or stuck in an all-night work marathon, the way they'd been all too frequently. They weren't even in the same room together. Blake was calling her from Red Rock, where he was on what she'd assumed was a vacation or some kind of family emergency.

Ever since the tornado had ripped through Red Rock she'd been watching the news reports religiously and reading everything she could get her hands on about the devastation that had befallen the idyllic Texas town where her childhood friend Wendy had taken up residence.

When the tornado had initially hit, a news bulletin had interrupted the program that was on TV. As she'd watched and listened, her whole world had ground to a halt. She'd wanted to attend Wendy's wedding, but because of circumstances, she'd had to remain in the office, manning her post, so to speak.

Her heart had all but stopped as she'd listened to the bulletin. She knew that Blake and Wendy, as well as the rest of their family, were all out there, stranded and in the tornado's path. The very thought unnerved her. She'd instantly started praying and searching for more information.

At one point, she had almost torn out of the office to try to get the first flight out to Red Rock, but no flights were going out to Red Rock, not directly or with layovers. Moreover, as reports began to come in, apparently there no longer was an airport for the flights to land in. The tornado had taken care of that.

That first day, she'd stayed up over twenty-four hours, scouring the channels and the internet, searching for any shred of information. Looking for the names of those who hadn't made it—desperately praying she wouldn't see any she recognized.

Especially not the name of the man she had loved with all her heart since she was a little girl.

Not that Blake Fortune actually ever noticed her. Oh, he'd seen her, but never as what she wanted him to see. To him she was just his sister's friend, the annoying girl next door. Later on, he'd acknowledged her as a college graduate with a marketing degree and he'd been impressed enough with her skills to hire her. But he never saw her as what she was. A woman who could love him the way he desired to be loved.

Still, something was better than nothing, so, as a kid she'd settled for his teasing words, his pranks, pretending indignance and secretly loving the attention. *Anything*, she had long ago decided, that had Blake looking in her direction was fine with her.

After she grew up, of course, she'd wanted more. Couldn't help wanting more. She'd wanted him to look at her as something other than Katie Wallace, the little girl next door.

That was why she'd gone to college to get that marketing degree in the first place. This was the key to getting closer to him, if not in his private life, then in his professional one. She'd nurtured the hope that if she worked really hard and proved to be indispensable to him, Blake would eventually wake up one morning to realize that he had feelings for her beyond his role as her boss.

That had been her plan, but even so, right now she still was having trouble believing that she wasn't dreaming. Was Blake actually saying what she thought he was saying?

After all this time?

Her heart was hammering in her throat as she forced out the words, "Excuse me?" into the receiver, scarcely above a whisper. She cleared her voice and spoke up. "Could you repeat please that?" Then, in case he thought she was being coy instead of just shocked, she quickly explained, "There's interference in the line, I didn't really hear what you just said."

"I said I need you," Blake told her, raising his voice. "It looks as if I'm going to be here longer than I thought. At least a couple of weeks, maybe three. When can you get out here?"

Katie allowed herself to savor his words for exactly thirty seconds. Where were Dorothy's magic ruby-red slippers when you needed them? she thought. Because then all it would take was clicking her heels together three times and she would be there at his side. Just the way she desperately wanted to be.

She knew that this had to be about work and that Blake needed her to get things done, but she viewed the phrase he'd uttered as her first step in the right direction. Someday, she promised herself, Blake was going to realize that he really did need her—and not just as his assistant.

"I can be on the first flight out there," she promised. Even as she spoke, she began searching the internet, pulling up the various airlines and looking at departure times. "I'll call you back the second I'm booked."

"That's my girl," he said. "I knew I could count on you."

That's my girl.

The three words echoed in her head over and over again as she all but flew back to her apartment and set a new world record for packing quickly.

That's my girl.

Definitely in the right direction, she thought happily.

Chapter 2

"You sure you don't mind me setting up an office in your house?" Blake asked his older brother Scott for a second time.

Ordinarily, he would have opted to use one of the offices in the building housing the Fortune Foundation in town. However, it was currently off-limits since it had sustained major structural damage during the tornado.

Scott had only recently decided to transplant himself from Atlanta to Red Rock and had just purchased a ranch and the house that stood on it. As of yet, he and Christina, the woman who had won his heart, were redecorating the rooms and several were still in limbo. Blake was temporarily claiming one for an office—as long as Scott had no objections.

"I mean, I'm already in your hair, bunking here until Wendy's baby is strong enough to finally make us uncles." Blake thought for a moment, then decided to ask Scott, since he was now the Red Rock resident. "Maybe it'd be better if I rent a couple of rooms in town—"

Scott waved away what he anticipated was the rest of his brother's thought.

"After the tornado, whatever's available in Red Rock has most likely been commandeered for temporary living quarters for the folks who lost their homes, or whose homes are so damaged that they're not safe to stay in right now. Besides," Scott added as an afterthought, "turning part of my place into 'FortuneSouth-West' might just make points with the old man, though I doubt it."

Their father, as everyone knew, had very high standards, which at times, Scott couldn't help feeling, even God might have some trouble reaching. It didn't help matters that, in the aftermath of the tornado, Scott had decided not to go back to Atlanta but to make a life for himself here, with a woman he firmly believed was his soul mate. A woman he had only known for a little over a month. The senior Fortune, Scott felt certain, undoubtedly believed that he had lost his mind—instead of finally finding his soul.

"And you're sure I won't be in your way?" Blake probed.

This new, improved and far more relaxed Scott was going to take some getting used to, Blake thought. Up until a month and a half ago, Scott had been as big a workaholic as their father and oldest brother, Michael. But he was definitely of a mind that this change in his brother was for the better.

"Not unless you plan on lying in the front doorway like a human obstacle course," Scott answered. He grinned as he regarded his brother who, at twenty-seven, was five years younger than he was. "Might be kind of nice having you around for a while. Aside from that little buried-alive incident on New Year's Eve-eve— and, of course, Wendy's wedding—we don't get to see each other all that much anymore," he noted.

The observation amused Blake. "Said the workaholic," he interjected.

"Not anymore," Scott emphasized. "That tornado kind of made me reexamine my priorities." Almost dying did that to a man, Scott thought. He felt as if he'd been given a second chance for a reason—and he didn't intend to waste it by going back to "business as usual."

"There's a lot more to life than finding different ways to continue building up a telecommunications empire."

His brother really was sincere, Blake thought. This wasn't just a passing phase. Scott was serious about putting his roots down in Red Rock because living here was so important to Christina, his future wife, and thus, important to him.

"Yeah, I know what you mean, about reexamining my priorities," Blake explained when Scott raised a quizzical eyebrow. "I told Wendy that I feel like my life's been on hold long enough and that it's time I did something about it."

"Anything you care to share with the class?" Scott asked, amused at the very serious expression on Blake's face.

"I'm going after the one who got away," Blake told him simply.

Scott nodded and smiled. He might have been a dedicated workaholic when they were all back in Atlanta, but that didn't mean that he had been wearing blinders 24/7. He was quite aware of how his young brother's assistant, Katie Wallace, looked at Blake when she thought no one was paying attention. At the time, he'd found it rather amusing. But now, finding himself on the other side of love, he understood how she must have felt—and continued to feel. But something wasn't making sense, he realized.

"I wasn't aware that she had exactly 'gotten away,'" Scott commented.

Blake supposed that Scott was either too busy to have noticed, or maybe he'd just forgotten. "Yeah, she did," he assured his brother.

Okay, maybe he'd missed a chapter or two of Blake's life, Scott thought. "So you're going after—"

"Brittany Everett, yes," Blake said, filling in the name for Scott.

For a second, all Scott did was stare at him. And then he murmured, "Oh," more to himself than to his brother.

"What do you mean, 'oh'?"

There was no point in talking about Katie if his brother's sights were set on a vapid prima donna like Brittany Everett. Like everyone else in the family, because of the circles they all moved in he was vaguely aware of the woman—and what he knew, he didn't find very compelling.

Scott shrugged, dismissing his slip. "Nothing, just surprised that you seem so determined to get together with her." For a moment, he thought back to his brother's college days.

"Didn't Brittany dump you right after graduation?"

"No one dumped anyone," Blake insisted. "We just drifted apart."

"Right, after you caught her in a lip-lock with some other guy, if I remember correctly."

"I should have fought for her."

You should have cut her loose long before that, Scott thought. But Blake was a big boy now, able to make his own decisions. Besides, Scott had a feeling that the more he talked against Brittany—whose only attributes as far as he could see were strictly physical— the more, he was certain, Blake would dig in. They were alike that way, he and his brother.

So Scott dropped the matter, stepped back and hoped for the best. "If you say so. Look, I promised Christina I'd meet her for lunch, so I'd better get going. Good luck with whatever it is you're planning to do." *And I hope you come to your senses real soon.*

The reference to time had Blake looking at his own watch. "Hey, I'd better get going, too. I've got to drive over to San Antonio International Airport to pick up Katie," he said, joining his brother in the hallway. "She's flying in to help me with my strategy to win back Brittany."

Scott stared at him, utterly stunned. "She

is?" he asked. This couldn't be right. "You actually told Katie that you were 'launching' this so-called campaign to get Brittany to become Mrs. Blake Fortune?"

"Well, not in so many words," Blake admitted. The next moment, he saw a very wide smile curving his brother's mouth. He was unaware of having said something funny. "What?"

"Nothing," Scott answered, waving his hand and struggling to keep the laughter under wraps. "Just, good luck with that." And then, he couldn't resist asking, "By the way, how many pallbearers would you like at your funeral?"

Maybe the tornado had shaken Scott up more than anyone realized, Blake thought. His brother wasn't making any sense. "What's that supposed to mean?"

But Scott continued grinning mysteriously. And then he patted him on the shoulder. "You'll figure it out, Blake," he assured him, just before he hurried off down the hallway and out of the house.

Blake shook his head as he followed slowly in his brother's path, heading for the car he'd left parked in the huge, circular driveway. He put the odd conversation with Scott out of his head.

Right now he had something more pressing to attend to.

The way he figured it, if the flight from Atlanta arrived on time, he was just going to make it to the airport by the skin of his teeth—barring the unforeseen. It was a footnote that he had gotten into the habit of adding ever since the tornado had turned his life and his family's lives entirely upside down, tossing them on their collective ears.

Katie had deliberately brought only carry-on luggage with her. She had no desire to spend the extra time required to wait for luggage.

So, in the interests of speed and efficiency, Katie had stuffed into a single piece of luggage everything she felt she would need that couldn't be purchased at some local shop between the airport and Red Rock. After engorging the suitcase to the point that it looked as if it would explode, she'd sat on the lid and fought with the zipper until she'd managed to bring the closure full circle.

She managed to secure the very last ticket for the next outgoing flight to San Antonio International Airport.

She didn't relax the entire flight, her mind busily embracing the key phrase Blake had used when he'd called her.

I need you.

Part of her still didn't believe she'd finally lived to see the day when everything she'd dreamed about for so long would actually start happening.

Don't start sending out the wedding invitations yet, her mind warned. That was the part of her that was still waiting for the other shoe to drop.

She could warn herself all she wanted about not getting too excited—but she still was.

When the plane landed—reasonably on time for once, she noted, hoping that was a good omen—she was debating whether to just rent a car and drive to Red Rock or splurge and have a shuttle service do the driving for her.

The latter would prove to be the more expensive route, because of the distance that was involved, but she really wasn't too keen on driving by herself all that way. She was tired and the prospect of falling asleep behind the wheel was unnerving.

Maybe if she had a really strong container of coffee—

As it turned out, there was no need to debate the pros and cons of driving versus being driven, because, as she was weighing her options, she realized that she was being paged over the P.A. system.

Heading over to the customer service desk, she didn't actually see Blake, she saw his smile. But she knew that smile even at this distance. It belonged to Blake. Blake was here! And he was walking toward her.

Reviewing their phone conversation in her head, she couldn't recall him saying anything about picking her up at the airport. She knew where he was staying, thanks to the directions he'd texted to her on her phone. Scott Fortune had bought a ranch here and Blake was staying with him. Since, according to Blake, the company would be paying for her flight, she'd just assumed that she would wind up charging either the car rental or the shuttle service to FortuneSouth Enterprises. Never one to wantonly spend money, even if it was someone else's, she was just trying to make the best decision.

Was Blake this eager to see her that he had driven over himself?

The pounding of her heart went up another notch.

The exhaustion that had been slowly laying claim to her completely vanished as Katie picked up her pace, all but breaking into a run as the distance between them shortened noticeably. The heavy suitcase became nothing more than an unwieldy pull toy in her wake.

"You made it," Blake called out to her, obviously pleased at how quickly she'd managed to get here after he'd called her.

Katie beamed at him. "Nothing could have kept me away."

"Good," he pronounced with approval. "Then we can get right down to work as soon as you're ready. Here, let me take that for you," he offered, putting his hand over hers on the suitcase handle.

The brief contact still managed to steal her breath away, as it usually did. But what he'd just said pushed reality in, front and center.

"Work?" Her heart fell. Blake was still making noises like a workaholic. The hope that he would be just a little more laidback, a little more...*personal*...died a quick, bitter death.

Katie had a strange expression on her face. He took it to mean that she was experiencing a little jet lag. Maybe she did need to rest awhile, although he'd known her to work tirelessly when the occasion called for it.

"Yes. Work," he repeated. "That's the reason I sent for you. It was Wendy's idea, really. She thought you could help me get my campaign underway."

"Your campaign," she repeated numbly. Was this why he "needed" her? To work on some marketing campaign? Here? She felt confused. Even so, she sensed her slim grasp on happiness slipping away as her heart constricted within her chest.

"Yes. My campaign," he asserted, then added the damning phrase: "To win back Brittany Everett." Not seeing her face all but fall, he laughed a little self-consciously. "I know it's not exactly what you're used to doing, but I thought that if I went about winning Brittany back the way we go about landing an account for FortuneSouth Enterprises, then I'm almost *guaranteed* to be successful."

So this was what shock felt like, Katie thought. Shock, mixed with acute disappointment. Her pounding heart now felt like utter lead in her chest.

"And Wendy suggested you send for *me* to help you procure this woman?" she asked in disbelief.

"Not procure," he corrected, bristling at the word she'd used. "That makes it sound sordid." He didn't want Katie starting out with the wrong idea about this. Otherwise, she'd be no help at all and, he had to admit, he had come to rely on her shrewd instincts pretty heavily these past two years. "Brittany and I had a connection in college."

"Yes, I remember," she answered grimly as they made their way down the escalator to the first floor.

There was deep regret in his voice as he concluded, "And then I didn't follow through. I want to win her back. I'll be taking her to the Valentine's Day fund-raiser in Atlanta in a few weeks. That's when I intend to make my move."

Were they talking about the same woman? As she recalled, the woman was a little too Scarlett O'Hara for her taste.

"Kind of hard to get close to someone with that kind of a throng surrounding her," she recalled.

That, Blake thought, disturbed by Katie's comment, was an unwarranted, uncalled-for assessment. "It wasn't a throng," he protested.

"Okay, a swarm, then. Or maybe 'mob' might be a better word to use," she suggested crisply.

How could he? her mind cried. How *could* he think about getting together with a girl like that again? She'd never understood what had compelled him to get together with Brittany in the first place. Yes, she had what amounted to an almost-perfect body, but it was coupled with a completely imperfect personality for him.

They were outside the terminal now and approaching the valet's booth. Blake glanced in her direction as he gave the valet his ticket.

"I'm sensing a little hostility here," he noted.

"Just a little?" Katie muttered under her breath.

Blake cocked his head, bringing his ear a little closer to her. The noise level outside the terminal was even louder than it was inside, making it hard to maintain a conversation without resorting to shouting. And Katie hadn't shouted. Had he not seen her lips moving, he wouldn't have even been aware that she'd said anything at all.

"What did you just say?" he asked.

Katie was quick to shake her head. There was no point in arguing. "Nothing."

Besides, what did she expect? she silently upbraided herself. For the world to suddenly change? For Blake to suddenly wake up, come to his senses and see what was right in front of him? A woman who was willing to love him, flaws and all, for the rest of his life—for the rest of *her* life.

Leopards didn't change their spots and Katie couldn't believe that in the interim years a girl like Brittany Everett would become more compatible with Blake.

What was *wrong* with him? she silently fumed.

The next moment, she redirected the question toward herself. What the hell was wrong with *her*? Had Blake *ever* indicated that he had feelings for her that went beyond a boss appreciating his employee's work? Did he even indicate that he felt she went above and beyond the call of duty each and every time?

Well, that was her mistake, wasn't it? She did so in an effort not just to seem indispensable to him, but to have him suddenly look at her, *really* look at her and see her for the first time. See how good she was for him—not just for the company, but for *him*—and then maybe, just maybe, that could lead to something more.

The word *more* however had no meaning here—unless it was to indicate that she doubted if Blake could be *more* wrong in his choice of a future wife, which was where this whole stupid "campaign" was clearly going.

She couldn't do this, she thought. She couldn't go through with this. She couldn't be his master strategist, his Cyrano, to help him land a woman who would ultimately stomp all over the heart he was planning on serving to her on a silver platter.

Katie began to voice her protest, but then, before even a single word managed to come out, she changed her mind.

Blake was going to go through with this with her or without her and if she protested, he might just view it as being a case of sour grapes. But if she was there, at his side, helping him with this awful campaign, maybe it would finally hit him that she had all the virtues and assets that he, in his delusion, thought that Brittany possessed.

And, she added silently, if this all blew up on him, she'd be right there to help him pick up the pieces.

She'd be privy to every detail of his plan and with it all laid out for her, she would know how best to ruin his plans. And by ruining them, she would be able to ultimately save the man from embarrassment and making the mistake of a lifetime—if not the century.

And if, at the same time, she could get him to see that it was her all along who he should have been with, well, so much the better.

"Look, if I'm asking too much," Blake was saying, apparently having second thoughts about the wisdom of asking her to help, "then maybe you should—"

"It's not that you're asking too much," she said, cutting him off. "It's just that, well, I'm not sure if I'm exactly the right person for the job. This *is* a little different than the usual campaigns we work on."

"Of course you're the right person for the job. I mean, this is about what appeals to a woman. Brittany's a woman and so are you, right?"

She looked at him, a little stunned. "Is that a question?" she wanted to know. "I mean, really?"

"No, no, of course you're a woman. That's what I'm counting on."

He was either being exceedingly simple-minded—or insulting. She wasn't sure which bothered her more. "That all women are alike?"

He couldn't really explain why, but he had the feeling he was in over his head—and drowning. What was needed was a time-out so that he could gather his thoughts together and begin again.

Blake was more than certain that Katie was the right woman for the job. After all, someone as attractive as she was probably had guys making a play for her all the time. What sort of things made her reactions positively? That's what he needed to find out. He just had to find the right way to phrase this so she wouldn't think that, well, he was coming onto her. Because he wasn't. Even if, sometimes when she looked at him, he'd find something stirring deep inside of him. That was just a basic, *physical* thing, nothing more.

Taking a breather, Blake pulled himself back and refocused.

"Tell you what," he proposed. "Let's get you over to Wendy's. She's dying to see you."

At least someone was, Katie thought.

Chapter 3

"Oh my God, just look at you," Katie cried as she walked into Wendy's bedroom.

After everything she'd heard about Wendy going into premature labor, Katie had expected to find her friend pale and languishing in bed. Instead, Wendy looked just the way she always did: bright and animated, and very, very pretty.

Wendy's eyes crinkled the moment she heard the sound of Katie's voice. She shifted in bed, excited to finally see her old friend.

"I know, I know, I'm as big as a house," she lamented, only half kidding.

"I was going to say glowing," Katie corrected tactfully. Granted, Wendy looked a bit larger than she had the last time they'd seen one another, but nowhere near Wendy's self-deprecating description.

"But you *were* thinking that I looked as big as a house," Wendy prodded. There was no way anyone walking into the room could miss this "bump," which was currently the biggest thing about her.

Katie knew better than to argue. No one won arguments with Wendy. "Not a house," she insisted. "Maybe a little cottage." She held up her thumb and forefinger, keeping them about an inch apart.

With a laugh, Wendy held out her arms to her friend. Katie had always had a way of making her feel instantly better. Now was no exception. "Come here and give me a hug," she implored.

It was all the invitation that Katie needed. Bending over, she embraced Wendy, giving her a heartfelt squeeze and holding on tightly for a moment. She really was very happy to finally see her.

"God, I've missed you," she said fiercely, then, as she stepped back, she added in a lower, embarrassed voice, "I'm sorry I couldn't come to the wedding."

Wendy waved away the apology. "Being best friends means never having to say you're sorry," she said as if that was a given between them. And then she gave Blake an accusing look. "I know my slave-driving brother left you to hold down the fort."

"I take exception to the term *slave driver*," Blake protested. "And what can I say?" he added with a careless shrug. "Katie happens to be very good at her job." And because she was, he had been able to fly to Red Rock for an extended week to attend his baby sister's wedding along with the rest of his family.

"Oh, I don't know, maybe you could have said, 'Hey, Katie, since my sister's your very oldest, dearest friend, forget about the fort.'"

"It wasn't the fort that needed holding down," Katie told her. "We had a last minute problem with a customer demanding changes to a contract that was going out and someone in marketing was needed to handle it. I knew Blake didn't want to miss your wedding, so I volunteered to stay behind and deal with the client," Katie told her. "It was kind of my anonymous wedding present to you."

"And in a way, it turned out for the best," Blake pointed out. "If she'd come to the wedding, Katie would have been struck at the airport like the rest of us—and who knows? Maybe she would have even gotten hurt. The way I see it, maybe staying behind to deal with the client and smooth things out saved Katie's life."

Wendy rolled her eyes at his comment. "You're really reaching there, Blake."

Katie was nothing if not a born mediator and now was no exception. She sidelined any further discussion about something that couldn't be changed by redirecting the conversation to the present. "Speaking of the tornado, is Javier doing any better now?"

"He's finally conscious. It was touch and go for a while and I know Marcos was really worried that his brother might not come out of his coma." She pressed her lips together. "We still don't know how extensive the damage to his spine and legs really is. Right now, he can't move them, but the doctor said this could just be due to some swelling along his spinal cord. Once that goes down, he should be able to walk again." The key word here, she added silently, was *should*.

As if reading her unspoken thoughts, Katie said firmly, "Yes, he will." Like Wendy, she believed in positive thought, taking it a step further. Positive thoughts yielded positive energy.

Wendy beamed. Though far from a negative person herself, there was something exceedingly uplifting about the upbeat tone in her friend's voice. She caught Katie's hand in hers for a moment and just held on.

"God, but it's going to be good having you around," she said with feeling.

"Speaking of which," Katie said, looking at Blake, "you haven't told me where I'm going to be staying. I'd like to drop off my things—"

"At Scott's," Blake surmised, mentioning where he was currently staying. At the same time, Wendy was saying something entirely different.

"Why, here, with me of course." How could Blake even think she'd have her friend staying anywhere but with her? "Katie's going to be staying at my house," she said, reinforcing her initial words. "It'll make visiting so much easier."

He didn't get it. Sure, she and Katie were friends, but he was family. He and Wendy shared the same blood. This wasn't making any sense.

"She stays here but you just threw me out?" he protested.

"I didn't 'throw' you out," Wendy tactfully pointed out. "I 'moved' you out. There is a difference, and it's because you were hovering over me all the time. Besides—" she looked at Katie again, so thrilled that she had actually made it out here "—Katie and I have a lot of catching up to do."

Blake looked both hurt and insulted before he managed to hide it. "And you and I don't?" he asked.

"There's not all that much catching up to do, Blake," she said tactfully, and then reminded him, "You'd only been gone from here a little more than a week before you came back, remember?"

Still, he was family and Katie wasn't. "Not the point."

Wendy sat up a little straighter and caught his hand. "You *know* I appreciate you coming back out here again to keep me company, Blake, I just don't need to see you 24/7," she told him. She tried to sound as kind as she could, then quickly added, "And I won't be seeing Katie 24/7, either, because you're going to be working the poor girl to death most of the time." Switching gears, she looked at her friend and warned, "Don't let him work you to death, you hear? I don't care if he thinks he is your boss."

"I don't *think* I'm her boss," Blake pointed out. "I *am* her boss." What was that old saying? he tried to remember. Something about a prophet never being honored in his own town.

Caught in the middle, Katie thought it prudent to come to Blake's defense. "He's not a slave driver, Wendy. As far as bosses go, Blake's pretty good."

Blake inclined his head. "Thank you." And then he looked at his sister. "At least someone around here appreciates me."

Slanting a glance at Katie, Wendy smiled and shook her head, amused. *Obtuse*, that was the word for it, all right. "You, big brother, don't even know the half of it."

He had no idea what Wendy was referring to and chalked it up to the fact that pregnancy and the influx of all those extra hormones were making his little sister say some very strange things these days. Even more so than normally.

Maybe it was time to retreat for a little while. After all, it wasn't as if he didn't have things to do that would keep him busy.

"Yeah, well, I tell you what, I'll let you two catch up a little, the way you want, and I'll swing by Scott's place to check into a couple of things." He deliberately struck a courtly pose as he asked, "Will it be all right with you, your highness, if I come back here in, say two hours, and collect my marketing assistant?"

"That's entirely up to Katie," Wendy told him, raising her hands as if she had nothing to do with that sort of decision.

It took Katie a second to realize that the ball

was now in her court and Blake was waiting for an answer from her. "Fine," she told him with feeling, coming to. "Two hours will be fine. Sooner if you'd like," she added as an afterthought.

"You heard the lady," Wendy said, taking charge again. For emphasis, she waved her brother away from the bed and toward the doorway. She was dying for some alone time with her friend. There were things she just had to find out. "Come back in two hours."

Blake almost reminded her that Katie had said "or sooner," then changed his mind. He wasn't about to argue with Wendy, not about anything if he could help it. Not in her present condition. Heaven only knew what might send her into premature labor again.

"Two hours it is," he agreed. And with that, he left the room.

"Wendy, I—" Katie began, only to be abruptly stopped by the mother-to-be before she had a chance to say anything more.

Wendy was holding her finger up to halt any further flow of words. At the same time she cocked her head, listening to something other than the sound of Katie's voice.

Her eyes shifted back to Katie. "Is he gone yet?" she wanted to know.

"Blake?"

Wendy seemed to indicate that she wanted her question answered before another word was said between them. Katie stepped into the hallway to make sure that the man who could raise her body temperature with just a single look in her direction was nowhere in the immediate vicinity.

"Yes," she said, reporting back, "he's gone." Curious, she crossed back to Wendy's bed and asked her, "Why?"

Because she planned to talk about her big brother and she didn't want him knowing that, Wendy thought. Out loud, though, she merely said, "I just don't want him eavesdropping on girl talk, that's all." She made a request. "You're going to be doing me a huge favor, making sure Blake keeps busy while he's here. Otherwise, he'll find some excuse to be over here night and day, watching me as if he expects me to suddenly explode or something," she complained. Being pregnant made her feel hugely vulnerable, not to mention grumpy. She just couldn't wait to be mistress of her own fate again.

"Sure thing," Katie readily agreed. That was what she'd initially thought was going to happen, anyway. It was just the car ride from the airport that had thrown a monkey wrench into everything. "I just wish that the campaign he wants me to help him with actually had something to do with work."

Wendy looked at her, momentarily speechless. Blake hadn't— He couldn't have— Her brother could *not* have laid out his half-baked plan before Katie. Not *seriously*.

Could he have?

"Don't tell me that Blake actually asked you to—" Wendy couldn't bring herself to finish the sentence, but the look on Katie's face made that unnecessary. Wendy covered her face with her hands. "Oh, God, not even Blake could be that dense." But even as she said it, she mentally crossed her fingers.

The smile on Katie's lips was small and, when Wendy looked closer she saw that it was also rather sad.

"Oh, I wouldn't be putting any bets on that if I were you," Katie advised. "At least, not unless you're bent on losing."

Wendy just couldn't believe it. It was one thing to talk about the idea to her, but she would have thought that someone as savvy as Blake would have come to his senses shortly after he had hatched this stupid, half-baked plan of his.

Closing her eyes for a moment as she searched for strength, Wendy sighed. "Oh,

God, Katie, he actually *asked* you to help him win over that dreadful woman?"

"Well, I don't know about dreadful," she allowed loyally, although for the life of her, she was beginning to wonder how she could harbor these feelings for a man who seemed to so easily disregard the fact that she had any feelings at all. "But he did say he wanted me to help him with his 'campaign' to win back Brittany Everett."

Wendy rolled her eyes in frustrated exasperation. "To win her back, my idiot brother would have had to *have* her in the first place."

"Wait, I'm confused," Katie protested. "Didn't he and Brittany go together just before they graduated college?"

She remembered how upset she'd been when she'd found out that Blake was seeing the beautiful young socialite. Katie had felt as if her entire world was crumbling right beneath her feet. It had taken her a while to get over it and get her mind back on her studies.

"Blake may have been 'going together,'" Wendy corrected. At least she remembered things clearly, even if Blake didn't. "Brittany apparently forgot. Besides, there's absolutely no comparison between the two of you. You *have* a heart. I think Brittany has a mirror where her heart is supposed to be. While my idiot brother was recruiting you for this impossibly ridiculous mission, did he happen to tell you how he and the Magnolia Queen came to 'break up'?" Wendy wanted to know.

Katie shook her head. "He didn't go into any details, no."

"Then allow me to fill you in," Wendy offered, warming up to her subject. "They were at a graduation party and became separated. At some point in the evening, he started looking for her. He walked around, searching the immediate party area, and found her making out with another guy."

Oh, poor Blake, was all Katie could think. "He found Brittany actually kissing some other guy?" she asked incredulously. How could she have even *looked* at another guy if she knew that Blake was committed to her?

Wendy shook her head, completely disgusted with her brother's choice in women. "Personally, I don't understand why Blake would even want to be in the same room with her, much less take her back."

Wendy was missing one very obvious point, Katie thought. "Maybe because Brittany's pretty much drop-dead gorgeous."

Wendy raised her chin. "So are you," she insisted loyally.

It was Katie's turn to roll her eyes. "Oh,

come on, Wendy. I do own a mirror, you know. I know exactly what I look like."

Wendy shook her head. Katie was missing the obvious. She'd been such a dedicated soul and hard worker for so long, she didn't even remember how to use her feminine wiles, but that was all right. Wendy was devious enough for both of them.

"The only difference between you and that woman my brother *thinks* he wants is that she knows how to apply makeup to her best advantage." Wendy's eyes narrowed as she looked at Katie. "Nothing you can't learn," she told her emphatically.

Maybe, Katie thought, but not easily. And not quickly enough. "And while I'm busy learning how to make a silk purse out of a sow's ear, Blake and Brittany will be exchanging wedding vows," she concluded unhappily.

Wendy waved away the very notion. "Not in a million years, I guarantee it," she promised with deadly certainty. She knew the Brittanys of the world. They took up space and looked attractive—as long as no one was looking closely. Because what they had was superficial. What Katie had ran deep. Clear down to the bone.

The next moment, Wendy lapsed into silence as she paused, thinking the situation over—

and seeing the potential that had been staring them in the face all along. It might just work.

"You know..." Her voice trailed off as an idea began to take serious shape. And then Wendy smiled. Broadly.

Katie was on her guard instantly. "Uh-oh, I know that look." It was Wendy's crafty expression.

The woman was up to something.

Katie held her breath as she asked, "What are you thinking?"

Wendy beamed at her. "Just that my beloved big brother might have just given us the perfect opportunity to make him see just how desirable a woman you really are."

"Right!" Katie laughed, shrugging off the compliment. But Wendy was obviously not kidding, she realized. "All right, I'm listening. Just how does my helping Blake put together his campaign strategy to bag the elusive Brittany-bird make him suddenly see how supposedly desirable I am?"

"Not supposedly," Wendy insisted. "You have to start thinking positively, Katie, or this is never going to work."

"I can *think* downright unshakably, that still doesn't mean that I—"

Wendy dropped her bombshell. "He'll have to practice on you."

Katie blinked. Had she missed something here? "Excuse me?"

"All these moves he's going to make on Brittany, he has to practice on someone, polish them up on someone." To her it was a given. Rehearsals always helped attain the desired results. Wendy smiled at her. "That 'someone' is going to be you. Dinner—you, dancing—you, moonlight walks—you, seductive techniques—"

This time, it was Katie who halted the conversation, holding up not just a finger but a whole hand.

"I think I get it," she said, fighting a very real blush that was swiftly advancing up along her neck and splaying across her cheeks with the force of the evening high tide.

Wendy saw the blush and smiled with satisfaction. "Yes, I can see that you do. By the time we're finished—by the time *you're* finished," she amended with a smile, "my brother is going to forget that Brittany Everett ever existed."

Katie had her doubts about that, but she had to admit that she really liked the way it sounded. For now, she allowed herself to savor what to her was tantamount to an impossible dream. She figured it was the least she could do after Wendy had gone to all that trouble to come up with said plan.

Even if it wasn't going to work.

Chapter 4

"You know, if you were really concerned about me, you'd find a way to get me the hell out of here."

Javier Mendoza struggled to keep his voice from rising as he complained to his younger brother, Marcos. He'd finally been moved out of ICU into a single care unit, but the hospital walls were only so thick and his deep voice was the kind that carried.

There was a frustrated frown on his handsome face and he looked like a man who was just about to lose the last shred of what was left of his overtaxed patience.

Marcos sympathized with his brother. He knew how he'd feel in Javier's place, but there was just no way that his brother was leaving here, not yet.

"I *am* concerned about you, which is why I'm not going to help smuggle you out of here," Marcos informed him. There was an irrefutable note of finality in his voice that most people—except for his wife, Wendy—knew not to argue with.

But Javier wasn't listening to the sound of his brother's voice. He was too focused on his own exasperation. One minute, he was a virile, strong man in his very prime, the next, when he opened his eyes again, he'd lost a month of his life to a coma and had to train his body to do the very basic of life's functions. Things that most people took for granted—that *he* had taken for granted—were now challenges to him. His legs refused to obey him and that caused him no end of frustration—as well as scaring the hell out of him. The fear was something he wasn't about to admit to a living soul, not even Marcos.

Although he had a sneaking suspicion when he looked into Marcos's eyes that his brother already knew that. However, Marcos had wisely refrained from saying anything about it.

Marcos put a comforting hand on his brother's shoulder, which, he noted, was utterly stiff with tension.

"Look, Javier, you have to give these doctors a chance," Marcos urged. "They know what they're doing and they're a great deal more familiar with these kinds of...problems," he finally said, for lack of a better word, "than you are."

Javier's dark eyes narrowed angrily. "It's *my* body and nobody's more familiar with it, or how it's supposed to work, than I am," he insisted hotly. "Don't get all hypocritical on me," he warned. "They wanted to keep Wendy here and she put her foot down, so they gave in and you took her home—just like she wanted," his brother pointed out.

Marcos shook his head. "No, that was different," he countered.

"How's that different?" Javier demanded. He realized that his voice had risen again. Biting back his temper, he made a concentrated effort to lower his tone. "Because Wendy's your wife and I'm not?"

Marcos laughed shortly. "No offense, Javier, but you'd make a pretty ugly wife," he cracked, hoping to get some kind of smile out of his brother. He failed. "And it's different because we don't know how long Wendy would have to stay here before the baby is strong enough to be born. Wendy's four walls might have changed, but she still has to stay in bed day and night.

She still can't get up the way she wants to." Javier had averted his face, but Marcos pressed on. "Now that the doctors have brought you out of that medically induced coma, they have a timetable for you."

"I'm not interested in *their* timetable," Javier snapped.

In his place, Marcos knew he'd feel the same way. But he wasn't in his brother's place and it was up to him to calm Javier down and make him be reasonable.

"Well, you should be," he said firmly. "Trust me, those doctors don't want to see your ugly face here any more than you want to be here. But this is the place where they can help you, where they can work with you."

"There's nothing to work with," Javier retorted coldly, staring down at the two stiff limbs beneath the blanket. The limbs that refused to move. "Look, if I've got to stay here, okay, I'll stay here. Doesn't really matter anyway. But I want you to tell everyone to stop coming."

"Why?" Marcos asked, stunned at this new curve his brother had just thrown him.

"Because I don't want them to see me like this, that's why," he said through gritted teeth.

Ordinarily, because Javier was his big brother and Marcos had grown up looking up to Javier, Marcos would have backed away and not pressed the subject. But this situation didn't come anywhere near close to fitting the description of being "ordinary."

"Like what?" he wanted to know.

"Like half a man," Javier shouted. "There, I said it. You happy now? Like half a man."

"This is just temporary," Marcos insisted.

"How do you *know* that?" Javier challenged. "You saw some written guarantee? How do you know that?" he shouted again.

"Because I do, that's why," Marcos shouted back, then caught himself and lowered his voice. "Once the swelling on your spinal cord goes down, you'll fully regain the use of your legs—and even if you didn't," he insisted, "who you are isn't trapped in any of your limbs. You're not you because of your legs or your arms or any other damn body part. You're Javier Mendoza because of what's inside of you. What's *here*," he said, jabbing his forefinger into the middle of Javier's chest. "You understand me? So stop your complaining and start focusing all that energy on getting better."

"You've got some mouth on you, you know that?" Javier retorted, but his voice was a little softer now. "Marriage do that to you?" It really wasn't a serious question, seeing as how, even though Wendy was expecting their first child at apparently any moment, Marcos and she had only been married for a little more than a month. A month that he had completely missed, Javier thought in rueful frustration.

"No, the tornado did," Marcos replied quite seriously. "Now, I mean it. Stop complaining and just be grateful that you're still alive and that you have the opportunity to mend. Not everyone was as lucky as you," he concluded more quietly, grimly recalling that several people he knew had lost their lives in the disaster.

Feeling just the slightest prick of guilt, Javier shrugged defensively as he stared out the window. "Easy for you to say."

"Easy?" Marcos echoed in disbelief. It felt as if he hadn't slept more than five hours in the past five weeks. "Ever since that tornado hit and they dug you out, I've been trying to find a way to split myself in two, being there for Wendy and here for you," he elaborated.

"I was in a coma," Javier pointed out. "There was no need—"

"There was a need," Marcos interrupted with conviction. "We all took turns reading to you. And there was music playing constantly. Wendy thought it might help. Just because you were in a coma didn't mean you couldn't hear," Marcos insisted. "And besides running back and forth between home and San Antonio, I still had to put in time at the restaurant," he reminded his brother, referring to Red, the restaurant that he managed for his aunt and uncle.

It was also the place where he had first met Wendy. Although he and the youngest member of the Atlanta Fortune family hadn't exactly hit it off at first—and that, he now had to admit, had been entirely his fault—the restaurant still held a very special place in his heart. He wouldn't have felt right about neglecting his duties there and having the other members of the staff pick up the slack for him, even if this was an unusual crisis.

Javier continued to stare out the window. "Well, you don't have to feel obligated to come back here and give me annoying pep talks."

Marcos moved around the bed and directly into Javier's line of vision, getting between him and the window. He looked at him for a long moment. "You really want me to leave and not come back?"

Javier opened his mouth, about to say yes. But in all honesty, it wouldn't have been the truth. And he wasn't angry at Marcos and his "pep talk," he was angry at the circumstances that had put him here. So he sighed and looked down at his motionless limbs.

"No," he mumbled. "I don't really want you to leave and not come back. It's just that—"

"You're so damn frustrated," Marcos filled in for his brother. He nodded. "Yeah, I know where you're coming from. It's hard being patient with things we have no control over. But the doctor said that the swelling *is* beginning to go down, so that means that you *are* getting better."

"Ha!" Javier jeered. So far, he didn't feel any different. "Not anywhere nearly as fast as I'd like."

Marcos laughed. He knew Javier. His brother would have wanted to be completely healed—yesterday. "I don't think that would be humanly possible, unless you had healing properties like Wolverine," he amended, thinking of the comic series he and his siblings used to read when they were children.

The mutant he was referring to was a favorite of *his* and Javier's. He'd never admitted that he had gravitated toward Wolverine *because* Javier liked the character as much as he did. Back then, he'd wanted to be exactly like his brother. Looking back now, he realized that what he'd had was a pronounced case of hero worship.

Childhood heroes shouldn't have to be talked out of making dumb mistakes, he thought, looking at Javier now. His brother should have better instincts than that.

"Just try to take it easy," Marcos advised. "Listen to the doctors and try to make gains during the physical therapy session—no matter how small," he urged. "Before you know it, this'll be behind you. I promise," he added, crossing his heart the way they used to as kids.

Javier looked totally unconvinced. He looked like a man who was struggling to make peace with a life sentence. "Yeah, right."

"Unless you've found a way to make time stand still." The phrase, which he'd just plucked out of the air, made him smile. Wendy had done that for him, he realized. She'd made time stand still.

Not at first, of course. At first she'd made time sizzle because she'd been so maddeningly infuriating and he'd been saddled with her. He'd perceived her as a so-called poor little rich girl—slumming in the working world until she grew bored. Her parents had sent her off to Red Rock, and then to their friends, his uncle and aunt, in hopes that somewhere along the line their youngest born would develop a work ethic.

They'd had no idea that they were sending her out to meet her destiny.

And seal his.

Still frowning, but appearing just the slightest bit contrite now, Javier looked at him. "Yeah, I suppose you're right."

"Happens every once in a while," Marcos told him good-naturedly, with a laugh. He glanced at his watch. It was getting late and he was falling behind schedule. Again. "Look, I've got to get going." He put his hand on his brother's shoulder. "Promise me you're not going to do anything stupid."

"You mean like disguise myself as an orderly and sneak out of here?" Javier asked innocently. He saw Marcos's eyes grow wide. "Take it easy!" Javier laughed for the first time since before the tornado had hit. "I was only kidding. If I tried to sneak out as an orderly, I'd have to do it snaking my way out on my hands and knees, like a soldier trying to crawl through an open field under the enemy's radar. Remember? I'm the guy whose legs won't listen to him."

Marcos still wanted assurances. "So you'll be here when I come back tomorrow?"

Javier preferred to leave it open-ended. "Unless the doctors change their minds about sending me home."

Well, there was absolutely no way *that* was going to happen in the next twenty-four hours, Marcos thought, but for the sake of his brother's abysmally low spirits, he merely nodded and repeated, "Unless they change their minds, right. I'll see you tomorrow," he promised, crossing to the door.

"Tell Wendy I was asking after her," Javier called to his brother.

Marcos turned in the doorway and smiled as he looked back at Javier. "I will," he told his brother. "She'll like that."

His wife, family rebel though she'd once been, was exceedingly family oriented these days, especially now that they were beginning a family of their own.

Once he was out of his brother's room, Marcos quickly made his way down the hall to the bank of elevators. He was a man in need of a miracle, he thought. Preferably one that caused all traffic to either disappear or conveniently part for him, so that he could get back to Red Rock and the restaurant at something akin to a reasonable hour.

He supposed that made him an unrealistic dreamer.

"It's a thirty-day plan," Blake told Wendy proudly the next morning. She'd arrived a few minutes before and he had brought her into the makeshift office he had put together in Scott's house.

He was still having some difficulty in think-

ing of his brother as a rancher and not a for-
ward-moving business dynamo. After all, he'd
spent all those years watching Scott and Michael, his oldest brother, constantly competing
with one another over absolutely everything
they laid eyes on, each always betting against
the other that he would be the winner.

How did someone go from that to a laidback man of the earth? It didn't seem possible
to him without involving stiff doses of tran-
quilizers.

Yet this was Scott's new life, one that he
was happily embracing—and all because of a
woman. The very woman he had been trapped
with when the tornado had all but buried them
alive in debris.

Well, if Scott could do an about-face and
turn his life completely around, Blake thought,
he certainly could launch a thirty-day campaign to win back the woman of his dreams.
The woman he knew in his bones destiny had
chosen for him, to remain at his side until
death parted them—and maybe even beyond.

"Then you really were serious about wanting
to go after Brittany and wear her down, like
any of our marketing customers," Katie said
as she sat down at her side of the desk. She'd
really hoped that once he'd slept on it—*really*
slept on it—Blake would realize how nonsensi-

cal that sounded and just move on. After all, it wasn't as if he didn't have any real work to do.

But obviously he didn't see it as nonsensical and he wasn't about to move on. Which in turn made it a problem she was going to have to deal with.

There were times when she fervently wished she didn't love the man as much as she did. But then, she might as well have wished that the sun wasn't going to rise the next morning. It really wasn't something that was going to happen anytime soon.

Or ever.

Blake caught the incredulous note in Katie's voice when she asked her question and, while he was convinced he was finally going about winning Brittany in the right way, he did value Katie's input. Over the past two years he had discovered that their onetime neighbor and his sister's childhood friend had an uncanny gift for putting things together and homing in on what needed fine-tuning.

He looked at her for a moment, trying to gauge what Katie had really meant. "You make it sound like I'm not playing with a full deck."

Katie shook her head. There was no way she was going to ever say something disparaging about him, especially to his face. There were times, when she looked around at other would-be applicants for her job, that she saw nothing but nubile, eager young women willing to do whatever it took to land a position. There was no way she could begin to compete against them on any level—other than demonstrating extreme competence. She was not about to do or say anything that would make Blake look for another assistant to take her place.

"Oh, no, the deck's full, all right—it's just a little different," she allowed, her voice trailing off as she frantically cast about for just the tiniest drop of the courage that she lacked.

His sister had insisted this morning that Katie go through with the idea that Wendy had come up with last night. She wanted Katie to strongly suggest that Blake try out each "step" of the plan on her first.

Katie sincerely doubted that he'd agree to that.

Here goes nothin'.

"You know," Katie began, feeling her way slowly around the words, trying her best to find the right ones, "since this plan of yours is such an unusual approach, maybe you should try it out first, you know, like a rehearsal or a dry run."

"Try it out?" Blake echoed. "I'm not sure I follow you."

Okay, she'd backtrack. "You want everything letter perfect, right?"

"Well, sure, that's the whole idea behind putting this down on paper and going over it," he told her, tapping what he had written on the eight-by-ten sheet of paper in the center of his desk.

"Having it down on paper doesn't give you a real feel for it," she told him, wondering at the same time where these words were coming from.

Was she somehow managing to channel Wendy? Because that would seem to be the only answer. She knew that, even under fire, she wasn't capable of coming up with these words on her own, not when *she* had so very much at stake here.

Blake leaned back in his chair, crossing his arms before him as he studied her face closely. "And what would?"

"If you practice all this on someone else first," Katie said a tad too quickly. "If you took that person—that *other* person—to this play—" she tapped the name of the play that Blake had selected "—before you took Brittany." She could see he wasn't on board with this yet. Katie pitched harder. "That way, you could see if it—the play—was the kind that she enjoyed seeing. It would be just awful if the show turned out to be something that she'd feel uncomfortable about seeing. You never know, Brittany might think you had intentionally dragged her to see it for some reason." Katie pressed her lips together, not knowing if she was getting through to him. Only one way to find out. "Do you understand what I'm trying to say?"

He smiled broadly and she felt her heart do a backflip. Seeing that smile on his face always had the same results.

"Yes, I do. You want to make sure this is all perfect for Brittany. You want me to succeed as much as I want to succeed." He took hold of her shoulders and pulled her to him, giving her what amounted to a fierce bear hug. "You really are something else, you know that, Katie? You're absolutely one of a kind," he pronounced.

When he released her, Katie had to concentrate in order to make the room stop spinning and settle back down on its foundation.

"Okay," Blake, won over, declared, "we'll do it your way, Katie. We'll put every piece of this plan to the acid test. Together. And we'll start at the beginning and work our way down."

She tried to keep her excitement from surfacing in her voice. He was going to be taking her out and they were going to be doing things together. Fun things. Never mind that she was acting as a stand-in. She was going to be with Blake all this time. And maybe, just maybe, somewhere in all that time, he'd realize that she was the girl for him.

"That way," she said matter-of-factly, while cheering on the inside, "if something doesn't work, you can substitute something else in its place and she'll never know."

He nodded, pleased as the plan began to gel and come together in his head. "Like I said, you really are one of a kind, Katie Wallace."

Yes, I am, and you're just too damn thick-headed to realize that on your own, she thought, even as she kept her easygoing smile pasted on her lips. *But you will, Blake Fortune, God willing, before it's all too late, you will.*

Chapter 5

"Dancing?" Blake repeated.

His tone was less than happy as he looked at Katie uncertainly. In an attempt to snag a little of his father's attention, he'd forged his way into his father's business world at an early age. Some things, per force, had been sacrificed and certain rites of passage never even approached. Consequently, learning to dance was one of those things that just had never happened for him. If he was completely honest with himself, he'd never felt that he'd missed anything by neglecting this tiny portion of his social education.

He nodded now at the list on his desk. At the time he'd printed it, he'd thought it was a final copy of his campaign strategy. Apparently, he'd thought wrong.

"Dancing never made my list," he pointed out. What with the play and other things, he felt that he had other ways to court the "Brittany Market" without having to resort to something that made him feel inadequate.

"I know," Katie replied simply. "But it should have."

She sounded pretty adamant, but Blake dug in his heels. He shrugged carelessly at the mere suggestion of being forced to move to a given beat. "It just seems so old-fashioned."

"Old-fashioned is good," Katie countered with conviction. The only way she was going to get through this, she thought, would be to focus on the concept that she was helping her friend reach his goal. If she allowed herself to dwell on her actual "motivation," then all bets were off. "Romance is old-fashioned, yet this is what you're really setting out to do, isn't it?" she pressed. "Romance Brittany? Sweep her off her feet?"

It was a rhetorical question and she hated the taste of every single word she was uttering. How she managed to talk and keep a forced smile on her lips, rather than hit him upside his head, was a credit to her strength of will.

"Yeah, but..." Blake's voice trailed off and

he looked at her, one friend putting his trust in another. "You're sure about this?" he asked uneasily.

"I'm sure," she answered with conviction. "Take her dancing."

Blake took in a breath. "But I can't," he finally admitted.

Katie looked at him innocently over the desk that was between them. "Can't take her?"

He shook his head. He hated admitting to any shortcoming, even something as trivial as dancing. "Can't dance."

She knew that. Just as she made it a point to know everything else about him—except why in heaven's name a man as intelligent as Blake Fortune seemed to be so obsessed with winning back an airhead like Brittany Everett. Everything about the woman was so shallow— were these the qualities he *really* wanted in a wife? Did he really only want eye candy to hang off his arm?

Katie refused to believe that. She *knew* Blake, and the Blake Fortune she knew liked having intelligent conversations on a broad spectrum of subjects. Brittany Everett could conduct an in-depth analysis on why the color mauve brought out the hint of violet in her eyes. Moreover, she could go on for hours about which of the newest Paris fashions were the most flattering to her figure and her porcelain complexion.

But neither were subjects *she*, Katie, could stretch out for more than thirty seconds—if that long—nor did she have any desire to do so.

Brittany just *couldn't* be the kind of woman he was interested in.

And yet...

And yet here they were, laying out plans that rivaled the complexity of Allied maneuvers for the D-day invasion on Omaha Beach.

Make the most of this opportunity, remember? If you teach him how to dance, he'll have to hold you in his arms in order to practice.

For a second, she could almost *swear* she heard Wendy's voice in her head, urging her on. She had to stop thinking about Brittany and just concentrate on the positive aspect here—she was spending a great deal of time with Blake, strategizing.

"No problem," she responded to his negative input with a wide smile. "I can dance and I'll be more than happy to teach you."

Blake continued to look at her with a doubtful expression. She obviously gave him too much credit, he thought. While he was a fairly decent athlete, he was convinced that he was in possession of two left feet when it came to being coordinated on the dance floor.

There had been one attempt to teach him—he vaguely remembered one of his sisters trying to get him to master the tango when he was in middle school—and that had been quickly aborted.

"Why don't we put dancing on the bottom of the list?" he suggested. Picking up a pen, he was about to do just that.

But Katie pulled the paper away from him and shook her head. "No. It's always a good idea to tackle the hardest project first. Isn't that what you always say?" she reminded him.

Blake nodded, none too happy about having his words used against him. "Yes, but I didn't expect it to come back and bite me. You really do listen to everything I have to say, don't you?" he marveled, impressed despite the situation.

She hung on his every word, but that wasn't something she wanted him to be aware of. So instead, she used work as an excuse. "You're the boss."

That he could use to his advantage, he thought. "Well, if I'm the boss—"

"Except for here," she quickly interjected before he could get rolling. Then, because she could see how frustrated he looked, she pointed out the obvious. "You did tell me you wanted my help, right?"

Part of him was beginning to have second thoughts about the wisdom of his having approached Katie with Project Brittany. "Right," he muttered.

"Well," she concluded brightly, "this is how I'm helping."

"By making me feel like an idiot?" he challenged, because that was how he was going to feel, tripping over his own feet and pretending it was called dancing.

She wasn't even going to try to argue that point. Instead, she just forged ahead. "By making you see that you really can be light on your feet." She looked at him and said softly, but with certainty, "You can do anything you set your mind to." She could see that he was weakening. "When your father put you in charge of marketing, didn't you tell me that you overheard him saying that he thought maybe you were in over your head?"

"Yes, he did," he recalled. He also recalled how good it had felt to prove the old man wrong—not that his father would ever admit it, of course. But it was enough that his father now knew Blake could handle it.

"And didn't you tell me that you used his belief that you were going to fail to make you work twice as hard, just because you wanted to prove him wrong and show him that you *could* handle whatever he threw at you?"

"You listen to everything I tell you?" He'd already said it once, but now he was completely floored by the realization that there was someone who actually did take in what he was saying. Not once in a while, but apparently all the time. It made him feel good.

"Pretty much," Katie replied with a dismissive nod. It was time to get this portion of the program underway, she thought. A ripple of anticipation undulated through her. "Okay, we're going to begin your first lesson right now."

"Now? Here?" Blake looked around. "Don't we need more room or at least to roll up the rug before we get started?" he asked. The makeshift office he'd set up was good enough to use temporarily, but it wasn't exactly spacious. Not like his office back in Atlanta. If they practiced here, they'd be bumping into furniture constantly.

"Scott and Christina are going to be out all morning," she told him. She'd already thought to check with Christina regarding their schedule for the day. "We can use the family room. It lets out onto the veranda." And she imagined them dancing across both.

"And music," Blake quickly pointed out,

raising another obstacle, one that he hoped provided more of a deterrent than the cramped quarters. He *really* didn't want to do this, even though he had to admit that she had a point. A lot of women did like to go dancing. "We need music, right?"

"Absolutely," she agreed.

He should have known that wouldn't be the end of it. Katie was opening her briefcase and taking out her iPod. She paused to hook it up to a deceptively small, metallic blue speaker.

Sensing he was watching her every move, she flashed Blake a triumphant smile. "Luckily, I came prepared. I have ballroom music on here," she told him, holding the small device aloft. "Tango, waltz, it's all here."

"You're kidding," he cried incredulously. It wasn't that he wasn't familiar with the capabilities of the gadget she had in her hand—he hadn't been living under a rock these last few years—it was just that he was surprised that her device contained something so tame, so classic as ballroom music.

Rather than refute him, Katie merely turned on the iPod, now hooked up to the single round speaker. One of Strauss's classical waltzes filled the air. He looked from the player to Katie. The woman was an endless source of surprises, he concluded.

"You always carry that around?" he wanted to know.

"My iPod? Yes. The speaker? No," she told him casually. "But I had a hunch you might need to at least brush up on some of your dance steps, so I put together a playlist on here for you," she confessed, holding up the iPod.

He'd been right to ask her help, he thought. The woman was exceedingly thorough and always seemed to manage to be ten steps ahead of him. He had a tendency to hang back if he felt uncomfortable about something and obviously, Katie had no qualms about kicking him in his complacency.

This was exactly what he needed.

Still, he didn't really like looking like a fool, even around an old friend who had never exhibited a judgmental moment in her life.

"Like I said," he murmured, "you really are one of a kind, Katie Wallace."

This time, Katie looked him squarely in the eye. "You're stalling."

He laughed. There was just no putting anything over on her. "I was hoping you wouldn't notice."

"I noticed," she informed him matter-of-factly. *I notice everything you do, everything you say. I notice everything about you.* "Let's go to the family room," she urged, leading the way. Blake had taken her on a quick tour of the house when she'd gotten here yesterday. She retained things like a human DVR, he couldn't help thinking.

Once she'd reached the family room, she quickly set up her iPod and hit the playlist she'd put together for him just last night.

"I thought we'd start out slow," she told him when the waltz filled the air. "All right, I'm sure you know this part," she said, positioning herself.

When Blake did as she told him to, Katie could have sworn she felt a warm shiver skittering up her spine, despite the fact that she was wearing very sensible clothes rather than the backless evening dress she imagined Brittany would be wearing for such an occasion.

She'd temporarily forgotten this part, Katie realized. That he would actually be touching her if they were going to get this dancing lesson underway. Every single time he touched her, she had the same reaction: a warmth would spontaneously ignite within her, sending out beams of light all through her like a winter bonfire on the beach.

Focus, Katie, focus, she ordered sternly. She couldn't allow herself to dissolve into a puddle. She had to get through this, had to act as if she was seriously going through the motions of teaching him to dance.

So that he could "seduce" Brittany, an inner voice taunted her.

"That's right," she said, as his hand slid around her waist, her mouth momentarily growing very dry. "Now take my left hand in your right one."

Though he was considered suave and charming, when he was out of his element as he as with these lessons, Blake felt that he bore a distinct resemblance to a lumbering bear.

"Like this?"

She smiled her approval. "Like that. Can't really mess that part up, seeing as how we both come with only one set of left and right hands," she teased.

He noticed that she seemed spunkier somehow and thought to himself that he rather liked this version of her. But then, he knew, there was nothing about Katie to dislike, at least he'd never encountered anything that had set him off.

"No, this part's easy," he contradicted, and then, in all fairness, he issued her a warning. "It's when I start stepping all over your feet that things are going to get rough."

"You are *not* going to step on my feet," Katie said firmly.

He raised one dark eyebrow as he regarded her. "You know something I don't?"

"Yes." She tilted her head up slightly, her eyes catching him. "I know that you're Blake Fortune and you can do absolutely anything you set your mind to," she told him, repeating the mantra she'd professed to believe earlier. Blake could be exceedingly stubborn when he wanted to be.

He sighed, prepared to give it his all—and hope that it was enough. "I wish I had as much faith in me as you seem to."

"No 'seem to' about it," she corrected with just the right touch of feeling. "I do." Well, now that he knew how to stand and what to do with his hands, it was time to let the games begin. She began to dance, but for the most part, Blake just stood there, his feet sealed in place. "All right," she urged, "now let the music talk to you."

He listened closer, but it was still the same. "There're no words," he protested.

"There don't have to be," she told him, then instructed, "*Feel* it." He looked at her a little blankly, so she elaborated. "Feel the rhythm, let it *seep* into your bones, into your system," she urged softly.

And then, strictly for his benefit, she began

counting off the steps between repetitive movements.

At first, he was concentrating so hard, listening to her counting and trying to follow each of her movements, that he didn't realize just how close her body was to his.

And then it dawned on him that he could actually *feel* every movement she made. The motions echoed against his body, urging him to mimic what was happening. And then the warmth began to sink in. Really sink in.

He felt the warmth of her body against his— or was that his against hers? He wasn't sure who was causing what. All he knew was that the end result was he could feel the heat, both from without and from within.

He caught himself looking at her. *Really* looking at her. And then he stumbled, stepping on her foot and the moment, he knew, was broken. As perhaps, quite possibly, was her foot.

"Sorry," he apologized as she stopped dancing for a second and paused to try to feel her toes. "I tried to warn you," he said defensively, looking very chagrined beneath the bravado. "I told you I wasn't any good at this."

"You can't expect to be perfect the first time out," she told him. She took a deep breath, willing the radiating pain in her foot to scale back so that she could continue. The last thing she wanted to do was hobble in front of him. That would definitely sideline him for the duration and that was *not* the plan. "Actually," she went on warmly, "you're doing a lot better than I thought you would at this point."

"Really?" he asked incredulously. It was clear from his tone that he thought he was doing rather poorly.

She nodded. He looked like a kid who'd just built his first soapbox racer, she thought. A huge wave of affection washed over her as she regarded Blake.

"Really," she told him. She could feel him slowing down, could see by the look in his eye what he was about to do—or not do—next. "Now, don't stop dancing," she urged with feeling. "That's the secret, no matter what happens on the floor—unless the iceberg hits, just keep on dancing until the song's over."

"Iceberg?" he questioned. And then, belatedly, he recognized the reference. "Oh. Right."

Her eyes were smiling at him as she said, "Right."

Maybe it was the music, or her encouragement. Or the fact that he felt as if he was finally getting the hang of this dancing thing, but Blake could feel a level of enthusiasm building within him. Enthusiasm and something more. Something…stirring for lack of a better word.

He supposed that it was just the simple fact that he was moving around an imaginary dance floor with a soft and supple body less than a half breath away from his. If he wasn't careful, things might begin happening that he didn't want happening. After all, he wasn't exactly made of stone and as for Katie, well, he'd be the first to admit—although not to her *or* to Wendy—that she was damn attractive. If he wasn't so consumed with winning back Brittany…

But he *was* consumed, he reminded himself. And Katie was just here to help him with that campaign. She'd probably be upset if she knew what he was thinking right now, he told himself.

With more effort than he thought it would take, Blake bank down thinking altogether and just focused on dancing, nothing more.

By the end of their first full "work" day, Katie felt rather triumphant. During the course of that time, she had taught Blake the fundamentals of several dances.

For the last one, when he looked at her mystified after she'd verbally run through the steps his feet were supposed to be taking, she'd placed his hands on her hips and then deliberately exaggerated their movement in time to the music. His eyes widened and as he continued looking at her, she could feel her own heart melting. Was he surprised that she'd become so brazen, or was there something else going through his mind? For the life of her, she couldn't tell.

Initially, her objective for doing what she just had was to help Blake absorb the rhythm so that he could begin to at least try to master this dance of lovers. However, she had a nervous feeling that she was the one getting trapped within her own web.

She just wasn't good at this, wasn't good at pretending she was some sort of a seductress. She was just a woman in love with a man who had held her heart captive ever since they'd been kids.

Blake knew Katie was just trying to help, but there was definitely something happening here besides his attempt to learn the steps of a dance that really had no place in his life. With his hands on her hips like this, he could feel their seductive sway and it was telegraphing itself throughout his entire body.

For just a split second, thoughts of sweeping Brittany off her feet slipped far into the background—so far that they were all but invisible. In the foreground was this new, troubling reaction he was having to his sister's best friend, to his marketing assistant—to a woman he had known almost as long as he had known himself.

This wasn't right. And yet, it was oddly tantalizing. He knew he should move his hands, mumble something about "getting it," and return to safer territory. But he let them keep dancing and let himself—just for this moment—continue the unexpected journey he suddenly found himself on.

How could he not hear her heart beating? Katie wondered. It was almost deafening. Feeling his palms spread out over her hips as she continued to move them in what could only be blatantly described as an open invitation was having one hell of a profound effect on her. She could feel every inch of her body reacting. Despite the throbbing music, time had suddenly and literally stood still for her.

Stood still while she found herself about an inch away from him. An inch away from his warm breath swirling along her throat and her face. An inch away from his mouth as he inclined his head ever so closer to her. Whether he was going to say something or had no idea that he'd reduced the space between them to nothingness, she wasn't sure, but she knew that being so close to him like this and not doing anything about it was become harder and harder for her.

Her heart was hammering so hard she was having trouble catching her breath. All she wanted to do was kiss him. Just touch her lips to his and taste them.

Just once.

But she knew she couldn't. She couldn't make the first move and if he chose not to make it, then there was no way she was going to allow herself to become embarrassed by taking the lead when he clearly wouldn't want her to.

Damn it, why aren't you kissing me? Can't you feel this? Can't you feel the electricity?

She struggled to regain control over herself. *You can do this, Katie. If you pass out at his feet, you're going to have to hand in your resignation, you know that. So get a grip!*

As Katie fought to center herself, she realized that she was also gripping Blake's shoulders for all she was worth. When he drew back his head to look into her eyes, she could see that he knew something was wrong.

Or, at the very least, that something was different.

Chapter 6

He forgot to measure.

The old adage, "Measure twice, cut once," the mantra of tailors, construction workers and exceedingly careful people who strove to avoid errors, had also been Blake's rule of thumb to a great extent. Because he worked for his father and knew that any mistakes he might inadvertently make would be greatly magnified in John Michael's eyes, Blake wound up applying the rule to every facet of his life. Which only seemed appropriate since most of his life of late was spent in the office.

But this time around he forgot to measure. He forgot to allow caution to guide him and had, for all intents and purposes, thrown that very caution to the proverbial winds and had gone, instead, with basic gut instincts.

One second he and Katie were trapped in a moment, mystified by the electricity crackling between them as seductive music played in the background, and the next, well, the next he'd brought his mouth down on hers and was kissing her.

Kissing Katie, not Brittany's stand-in, as he'd been regarding Katie all afternoon while they'd danced. Or rather, while she danced. As for him, he'd just shuffled and moved his feet, trying not to trip or pitch forward and embarrass himself. But during that entire—and at times rather awkward—time, he'd regarded Katie as just a placeholder for the woman he really wanted to hold in his arms. The woman he really wanted to sweep off her feet.

Brittany.

But the woman he caught himself kissing wasn't Brittany's stand-in. He had been drawn to Katie, was kissing Katie because he couldn't rescue himself from the swirling curiosity, a need, that had suddenly risen up, urging him on.

And the worst of it was, kissing Katie satisfied nothing. It certainly didn't put his curiosity to rest. Instead, it just seemed to feed some insatiable craving within him. An all-consuming craving he shouldn't have felt for so many reasons that it would have taken him the better part of an hour just to list them.

Any second now, Blake told himself. Any second now he would step back and end this. Step back from Katie and into what this was all supposed to be about—a detailed campaign to win back the woman of his dreams.

But since he was already kissing Katie, he gave himself permission to continue this small aberration a few seconds longer.

After all, what were a few seconds in the ultimate scheme of things? They were so insignificantly minuscule, they didn't even register.

They didn't even—

They didn't—

Pulling Katie even closer to him, so close that he was in danger of merging with her very essence, Blake lost the train of his thought and then just gave up trying to think altogether.

Oh God.

Oh God, oh God, oh God.

It had finally happened, Katie realized in a panic. She had finally cracked under the pressure of her own desire and was now hallucinating. She *had* to be hallucinating because this just couldn't be happening.

Oh, she'd *wished* it to happen, and ordinarily, wishing didn't make something so. But somehow, this time around, she'd cracked and fallen headfirst down the rabbit hole where dreams became reality.

Except, that just *did not* happen. Not in her orderly world.

And yet, here she was, kissing Blake, losing herself in Blake. And dreams had become a reality.

Her body felt as if it was on fire as she rose up on her toes, absorbing every inch of heat emanating from his rock-hard torso. What thoughts she had were rolling about in her head like so many scattered marbles, turning here and there with no rhyme or reason to their movements.

If this *was* a hallucination, she would be more than happily willing to continue existing in this Mad Hatter world. There was nothing in her own, even-paced world worth going back for.

Nothing at all.

Except maybe for Wendy, a tiny voice from somewhere on the perimeter of her consciousness whispered. Wendy, who needed her. Who needed a friend to hold her hand while she dealt with the complications of her first pregnancy.

With a superhuman effort, something she'd

never even suspected she possessed, Katie drew on all her strength to move her head back a fraction of an inch. Just enough to create a tiny bit of space between them. A tiny space that had all the characteristics of a huge, cold chasm.

The first words out of Blake's mouth made the temperature of that chasm even colder.

"I'm sorry."

She could feel her heart pulling into itself in her chest. Standing outside of herself, she heard this disembodied voice—hers?—ask, "For?" The single word came out as an all but inaudible whisper.

He read her lips more than heard her voice. Feeling incredibly alive and yet incredibly confused at the same time, Blake tried to give substance to his apology. Because what he'd done was take advantage of both Katie and the situation.

That just wasn't like him.

Was it? he wondered uncomfortably.

"For kissing you," he said out loud.

Stung by his apology, Katie did her best to appear unaffected and pretended to just shrug off the entire incident, which would be forever and indelibly burned into her soul from this moment forward.

"It's not like you branded me with a poker," she told him flippantly.

Except that in reality, that was exactly what had just happened. His kiss, the kiss that she had dreamt about for half her lifetime, had turned out to be a hundredfold better than anything she could have remotely imagined. Time had stood still while the earth moved and, as incongruent as that might have sounded to anyone, that was the only way she could even begin to explain what had just happened to her.

The last thing she wanted was to have him marring this for her with a stupid apology that was heavy with his regret. Maybe he was sorry about what had just happened between them, but she wasn't.

"Besides," she continued with studied nonchalance, "it happens. Don't give it another thought."

But I will, Blake realized. *That's just the problem. I will.*

Needing some distance, however minor, between them, she went over to the side table where she'd set up her iPod and the speaker, and shut them both down. As she deliberately kept her back to him, Katie did her best to sound chipper and completely in control—even though her knees still felt watery.

"I think that was enough of a dance lesson for one day."

"Yeah. Yes," he amended, then echoed, "Enough," much the way someone else might have cried, "Uncle!" Though he wouldn't have admitted it to anyone, he was still not quite able to focus on anything. His brain felt incredibly fuzzy. Feeling adrift, he grasped onto the one thing that had been established: their routine. "Um, why don't I drive you back to Wendy's place?"

Turning around to face him, Katie glanced at her watch. It was only a few minutes after three in the afternoon. Way before the end of an actual workday. He really was eager to get rid of her, wasn't he? she thought with a bitter pang.

"I could stay and do some actual work," she volunteered. "Something that I would get paid for during a normal day," she clarified.

There was no way he could get his mind on work, not immediately. Not after what had just happened. Why did he feel as if he'd just fallen out of a twenty-foot tree, while she was acting as if nothing had happened? Hadn't she been on the other end of that kiss?

Maybe he underestimated Katie's experience level, he mused.

"No, I think you earned the rest of the afternoon off," he insisted.

Definitely eager to get rid of her, Katie thought again. And then more thoughts—questions— began to assail her. Had the kiss been that bad? Or that good? She suddenly caught herself wondering. Because heaven knew that kiss had just knocked the foundations of her world out from under her.

Maybe, just maybe, he'd experienced a slight setback in his plans, as well. Why else would he send her away in the middle of the day?

The more she thought about it, the more it heartened her. Finally, after all this time, a toehold.

"All right." She gathered together the iPod and its accompanying speaker, depositing them both back into her briefcase. "If you don't mind driving me back, I'll be ready in a couple of minutes."

Finally looking at him again, she felt another shiver dancing up and down her spine. God, but the man was just too damn handsome for her own good.

"You might want to stay and have dinner with Wendy once we get there," she suggested.

"Won't that be hovering?" he asked, thinking of what Wendy had accused him of doing. That was still a very sore point with him.

Her mouth curved in a grin. "No, I'm pretty sure that's just called dinner." And then she grew a little more serious as she crossed back to him. "Wendy's very grateful that you rearranged your life so that you could be here for her while she's going through this trial-by-baby ordeal."

He checked his pockets for keys to both Scott's place and the rental he was driving. Right now, he wasn't all that certain about anything, but thankfully, the keys were in his left pocket. Taking them out, Blake led the way out of the house.

"She looked pretty annoyed with me the last time I saw her," he remembered.

Actually, Katie knew that Wendy had been downright angry because Blake was so consumed with the idea of going after Brittany, but Katie tactfully smoothed that over. "That's because she's worried about you."

"Worried?" he repeated incredulously. "Why would she be worried about me?"

Wendy was right, she thought. Men could be so thick sometimes.

"She doesn't want to see you hurt and she thinks that Brittany will rip your heart out and use it for a coaster." She paused for a moment, weighing the wisdom of saying the next part.

She decided to plunge in. "The way she did the last time."

"No, she didn't," Blake protested, instantly coming to the absent woman's defense. "We broke up because of a misunderstanding."

Katie looked at him innocently as she asked, "You misunderstood why she was lip-locked with another man when you'd brought her to the party as your date?"

He was far from happy that had gotten out. Annoyed, he asked, "Has Wendy been talking to you?"

Katie pressed her lips together. She recognized her misstep the second she'd made it.

Holding up her hands in surrender, she gingerly backed away from the topic. Men, Wendy had told her, didn't like having their faults and mistakes pointed out to them. Even the big ones. *Especially* the big ones. Having grown up without any siblings and not really having any sort of a dating life to speak of, her experience when it came to the games people played with one another was severely limited. She believed in honesty, but obviously not everyone always saw it as the best policy.

"Sorry," she apologized. "Not my business." She lowered her hands. "Maybe I just got my details wrong." She had almost said "facts" instead, but that too would have wound up bruising Blake's ego.

He was too good for the likes of Brittany, but she couldn't say that, either. All she could do was hope that Wendy's plan for her to distract Blake while supposedly teaching him how to win Brittany would ultimately work.

And if it didn't, if she did too good a job and actually helped him with this pursuit, well, at least she was going to have a wonderful time as the understudy.

It wasn't much, but then, she'd never really asked for very much, she thought as she got into the passenger side of Blake's car.

Glancing in her direction, Blake waited for her to buckle up, then took off.

There wasn't much conversation to speak of.

The moment Wendy saw her brother and Katie walking into her bedroom, she knew something had changed. She could see it in their body language. It was there, in the expression on her friend's face and definitely there in the rather shaken look in her brother's eyes.

Something had happened and she knew she wasn't going to be able to find out what until she could get Katie alone to question her.

And that, apparently, wasn't going to hap-

pen until after they had dinner. Blake, once
he started talking to her, gave every indication that he was more than willing to stay until
long after the cows came home.

She couldn't chase him off without really
alienating him. Frustrated, Wendy struggled
to find some kind of compromising middle
ground. It was everything she could do not
to burst while holding her questions in check.

So, the three of them had dinner in the room
that now held her a prisoner day and night.
Because of her condition, Marcos had hired
a housekeeper, a pleasant-faced older woman
named Juanita, and the woman had served
them a dinner that had come straight from
the kitchen of Red, the restaurant that Marcos managed. Marcos himself was there now,
which meant there were only the three of them
for dinner.

Less than halfway through the meal, Wendy
began to give the performance of her life, mur-
muring about how fatigued she'd felt all day,
but, as sometimes happened because she was
"stuck in bed," she'd been unable to really
sleep.

"But now, after having this meal that my
loving husband sent over from the restaurant,"
she said, pausing to stifle yet *another* yawn,
"I think I'll probably be able to drop off like

a brick." Her eyes shifted toward her brother. "If I fall asleep midsentence, you'll forgive me, right, Blake?"

"Better yet," Blake told his sister, shifting out of the way as the housekeeper collected the last of the dishes and cleared them away. "I'll get out of your hair and let you go to sleep." Leaning over the bed, he kissed Wendy on the cheek. "You get some rest and I'll see you in the morning when I swing by to pick up Br—eh, Katie." He looked at the woman who had unexpectedly set off such a chain reaction within him this afternoon. He was still trying to sort out just exactly what had happened and what it all ultimately meant. For now, he nodded at her as if everything was still the same as it had been just this morning. "I'll see you tomorrow, Katie."

Katie returned the nod, debating whether or not to walk him out, then deciding it was best if she didn't. The drive here from Scott and Christina's ranch had been a little awkward and forced. Both of them were careful to tiptoe around the elephant that was stuffed into the car with them. They both needed a little break to regroup, she thought.

Maybe by tomorrow, things would get back to normal—whatever that was now.

"Right, tomorrow." Even as she said it, she

could feel her lips tingling ever so slightly from the memory of this afternoon.

As both the housekeeper and Blake walked out of the room, she turned to look at Wendy. Giving her a quick, preoccupied smile, she told her best friend, "I'll see you tomorrow."

Turning to leave, Katie was surprised to hear her exceptionally sleepy friend declare in a firm, emphatic and no-nonsense voice, "You get back here, missy. You're not going *anywhere* until you tell me absolutely everything."

Turning around, she stared at Wendy. Three minutes ago, the woman had been all but wilting. "What happened to being so tired you were afraid you were going to fall asleep midsentence?"

Wendy laughed, clearly surprised that Katie hadn't seen through the act. "And you believed me?" she asked, amused. "I said that for Blake's benefit. I mean, I can't ask you questions about what's going on with him sitting right there, so I wanted him to leave. But I knew that if I asked him to, he's so sensitive, his feelings would really be hurt." She sighed, shaking her head. "Blake still brings up the fact that I said he was hovering every chance he gets." She shifted her attention back to Katie, whom she had expected to see through her little act immediately. "God, Katie, aren't you paying attention?"

Second-guessing was just not the way she usually operated. "I thought I was, but I guess that I obviously wasn't." Katie shrugged. "Sorry."

Wendy waved away the apology as she shifted closer to the edge of her king-size bed. She wasn't interested in apologies, she was interested in why both her friend and her brother had looked off center when they'd walked into her room.

"Okay," she declared, then ordered, "give."

Katie stared at Wendy, confused. "Give?" she repeated.

"Yes." Suppressing an exasperated sigh, Wendy carefully enunciated her request. "Give me the details. Tell me what happened." When that didn't prompt an immediate outpouring of information, Wendy elaborated. "You and Blake both walked in with really weird expressions on your faces, like you'd both been standing on a mountaintop, watching a sunrise when you clearly were expecting to see was a sunset. *What happened between the two of you?*" she repeated, this time in a far more firm, demanding voice. "Spill it. *All* of it."

Her eyes all but pinned Katie in place, where she was going to remain until she told her what she wanted to hear.

"I took your advice," Katie began slowly. "I started to teach Blake ballroom dancing."

Wendy winced a little at the image that conjured up. "Blake has two left feet."

"So he said. Actually," Katie admitted, "given what I thought was going to happen, he wasn't all that bad."

Wendy was still waiting impatiently for something that would explain the dazed expressions she'd seen.

"Okay, well, it wasn't his feet that put that stunned expression on your face," Wendy concluded. Her eyes narrowed. Her hormones had her emotions all over the map and patience was in very short supply. "Are you going to make me beg?" she wanted to know.

"Of course not," Katie protested.

"Then tell me!" Wendy ordered, surrendering the last shred of her quickly failing patience.

Part of Katie felt almost silly saying this at her age. The other part felt almost as if she was betraying Blake by telling tales out of school. It took her a moment to calm herself.

Then, taking a deep breath, Katie said, "He kissed me."

Wendy's eyes almost fell out of her head. And then, the next minute, she was grinning so hard her face looked as if it ran the very real danger of splitting completely in two.

Chapter 7

It took Wendy a second to collect herself. Her excitement over what was clearly a significant break-through for Katie and Blake was having an unexpected—and unsettling—side effect. She felt twinges, *strong* twinges that were reminiscent of what she'd experienced when she'd suddenly gone into premature labor.

Taking a breath in slowly, Wendy grasped the blanket on either side of her and offered up a silent prayer as she waited for the sensation to pass. Less than two minutes later—it felt like a lifetime and a half—it finally passed. But by then, she was perspiring and feeling somewhat light-headed. It took concentration on her part to keep the large room from spinning around wildly.

The next moment, she saw Katie peering at her face uncertainly. "Wendy, are you all right?"

Katie's voice seemed to echo in her head as she heard her best friend ask the question.

Wendy took another second before she answered. She didn't want to alarm Katie by sounding out of breath when all she was doing was lying here.

"I'm fine, Katie, just really excited about that kiss," Wendy lied. Wanting to get the focus back where it belonged, she pressed for some kind of details. "All right, Blake kissed you. Then what?"

Katie wasn't sure just what it was that her friend wanted to hear. "I kissed him back."

The contractions, now gone, took a backseat to impatience. "And?"

"And it was wonderful," Katie confessed wistfully. Her words were accompanied by a heartfelt sigh.

Wendy knew Katie too well to think her friend was trying to be coy or draw things out. Katie obviously didn't understand what she was asking her. So Wendy verbally sketched an outline and waited for her to fill it in. "And what happened after he kissed you and you kissed him back?"

The rise and fall of Katie's slender shoulders was guileless. "We came here."

Wendy enunciated each word through gritted teeth. "And nothing in between?"

"Well, yes," Katie conceded. It was a given, since she hadn't rented a car here, but nonetheless she added, "Blake drove."

Wendy pressed her lips together, suppressing a guttural sound of pure frustration. Pinning Katie with a look, she knew very well that her best friend wasn't teasing her—she was dead serious in her recitation. Clearly there were some things missing from Katie's education, despite her graduation from a top university with honors.

There was no delicate way to ask, so she didn't bother trying. Instead, Wendy bluntly asked, "Katie, do you know how to flirt?"

A defensive look crept into Katie's normally warm brown eyes. "Flirting wasn't a prerequisite for my degree."

Well, that answered that, Wendy thought. She'd thought that perhaps, because it had been a while since she and Katie had seen one another and people did change—she was living proof of that, transitioning from a party girl to a doting homebody—that Katie had developed some feminine wiles. Obviously she hadn't, but that was okay. That was what Katie had her for. "So the answer's no." Wendy shook her head and struggled to suppress a sigh. "Settle in, Katie," she instructed, pointing to the edge of her bed. "You and I have work to do."

Katie's radar went up. Wendy was going to try to change her and, while that kind of a breezy, flirtatious manner suited Wendy to a *T*, it just wasn't her, Katie thought. Wendy could effortlessly have men eating out of her hand— before she'd met Marcos, she'd *had* men eating out of her hand.

But flirting to Katie meant leading someone on just to satisfy her own ego—if she actually had one—and she didn't see the point of that. Still, she didn't want to sound ungrateful.

"Wendy," she began a little hesitantly, "it's not that I don't appreciate what you're trying to do for me, but—"

Wendy was very good about reading between the lines and knew where her friend was heading with this. However, the sad fact of life was that nice girls did finish last more times than not, and a little something extra to help tip the scales never hurt. She knew just what to say to make Katie come around.

"You'd rather he wound up with that spoiled Southern belle?"

Katie shook her head. Brittany would just use Blake all over again. They both knew that.

"No," she said with feeling.

Wendy had expected nothing else. With a smart nod of her head she declared, "All right then, case closed. You're learning how to flirt."

It was obvious Katie had no choice in the matter—there was no known record of *anyone* ever winning an argument with Wendy, at least not directly—so Katie surrendered. She settled in and listened to what her friend had to say. She had no intention of putting anything she was about to be told to any active use, but listening to Wendy was a great deal easier than arguing with her and refuting anything she had to say. So, in essence, Katie silently chose to take the high road.

Mercifully, Wendy was brief and succinct. The lesson involved mastering alternating looks of adoration and out-and-out sexy expressions. There was also mention of a sexy walk, complete with a gentle, come-hither swaying of the hips, but since Wendy was bedridden, the instructions were all verbal rather than visual.

And just when Katie thought Wendy had exhausted her subject, her friend suddenly pounced on the topic of clothing.

Pressing her lips together, Wendy looked reprovingly at what Katie was wearing. "Does everything you packed look like that?"

Caught off guard, Katie looked down at what she had on. It was a navy blue skirt with a matching jacket, beneath which she had on a light pink blouse. It was crisp, subdued and professional. Katie saw nothing wrong with it.

"What's wrong with what I'm wearing?" she wanted to know.

Wendy didn't want to hurt her feelings, but there was a great deal at stake here—for all three of them. If Blake hooked up with Brittany, Katie would be heartbroken and Wendy herself would be in danger of being sent away for justifiable homicide. Brittany had *always* rubbed her the wrong way.

And then, of course, down the line Blake would be dumped and his ego would take a beating, never mind his heart. As far as she was concerned, it was crucial that Katie win this battle for her brother's affections.

"Nothing," Wendy agreed, "if you're bucking for Marketing Assistant of the Year. But if you want to be noticed as a woman, you need something softer and maybe just a tiny bit slinkier."

"I came to work, Wendy," Katie pointed out, "not to slink."

Wendy's eyes met hers. "Yes, but the 'office' is a room in my brother Scott's ranch."

Katie had no idea where Wendy was going with that line. "What does that have to do with anything?" she wanted to know.

"Blake improvised," Wendy pointed out. When the light apparently didn't dawn for Katie, she added, "You do the same." She could see she still wasn't getting through. Or, if she was, then Katie was resisting what she was being told. Wendy pointed toward the double doors on the other side of the room. "Open my closet, please," she instructed.

She didn't want Wendy's clothes. She liked her own just fine. "Wendy, I—"

"Don't argue with a pregnant woman." Wendy pointed toward the closet again, this time more regally, like a queen commanding her servant. "Open my closet," she repeated more firmly. "You and I wear the same size, or did before I became as big as a house," Wendy observed ruefully. She wanted this baby desperately. Loved this baby desperately. But she absolutely *hated* being pregnant. "Pick out something more feminine."

"Why?" she asked warily.

"Just do it," Wendy ordered wearily. "If I can't get you to flirt—and don't bother denying it," she interjected quickly, "I can tell by the look in your eyes that you're not going to do a thing I just tried to teach you to do—I can at least get you to stop hiding how pretty you actually are."

Now that just wasn't true, Katie thought. Where did Wendy get these ideas? "I'm not hiding anything," Katie protested.

Wendy didn't want to waste time waltzing around words. "All right, not setting your features off to their best advantage. Better?"

This was all useless, Katie thought. If Blake didn't want *her* as herself, then maybe there was no point in pursing this any further. She couldn't maintain a facade indefinitely, even if it meant having Blake in her life instead of his daydreaming about the likes of Brittany.

"Wendy—"

Knuckles digging into the mattress on either side of her, Wendy drew herself up in her bed.

"Do I have to get up and find clothes for you?" Wendy wanted to know. "Because I will." To illustrate her point, she threw back the covers from her bed and began to swing out her legs.

"Stop!" Katie cried. Hurrying over to Wendy, she pushed the covers back over Wendy's legs.

Wendy suppressed her triumphant smile. Instead, she calmly ordered, "All right, then you go and select some decent clothes. Just remember, if you win over Blake, you'll be doing me a favor. Because if Blake gets that woman to go out with him, and—God forbid—marry him, I'm going to have to kill her and then my baby is going to grow up with a jailbird for a mother."

Katie couldn't hold back her laughter. "When did you get so melodramatic?"

That was simple enough to answer. "When you started being so stubborn."

Katie relented. "Point taken. Okay, I'll pick out something."

That wasn't enough to convince Wendy. She wanted more of a commitment. "And wear it?"

With a sigh, Katie nodded and gave her word. "And wear it." Like a soldier on a forced march, she opened the closet doors and disappeared into its depths.

Only then did Wendy begin to relax. Katie never lied. "That's my girl."

"Maybe I should just wear a bikini to work tomorrow," Katie said sarcastically, her voice drifting out from inside the closet.

"Wrong season," Wendy pointed out matter-of-factly. "It's too cold for that. Otherwise, that would be a good solution."

Katie peered out to see if Wendy was serious. Her expression made it impossible to tell.

"Pick five outfits and bring them out," Wendy instructed. "So I can rank them."

Katie rolled her eyes. Wendy, apparently, was in full battle mode and dead serious. There would be no negotiating, no arguing with her. Resigned, Katie went back into the closet to find her battle armor.

"Have I seen you in that before?" Blake asked Katie the following morning. Picking her up for another day of strategizing amid a smattering of actual work, he'd been in the middle of talking as he led the way back to his car when he'd abruptly stopped and really looked at her. If the expression on his face was any indication, he was scrutinizing every inch of her.

"No," Katie answered quietly. Tossing her purse on the passenger floor, she got into the vehicle.

"Oh." He slid in behind the steering wheel. "Reason I asked is that it looks familiar."

She was wearing a long-sleeved, turtle-necked turquoise dress that lovingly adhered to her curves—and ran out of material about four inches above her knees. Like most of Wendy's clothes, it was an outfit that was intended to make a man sit up and take notice.

It was on the tip of her tongue to own up to

that, but then she'd be forced to explain why she was wearing his sister's clothes. She didn't believe in lying and, anyway, she wasn't good at it. But telling him the real reason she was wearing this and had in her closet other bright, sexy outfits that his sister had made her borrow, well, that was just too embarrassing for words. To spare both of them, she went with a creative, evasive version of the truth.

"No," she said innocently, avoiding his eyes, "I've never worn this before."

Blake nodded absently, taking the information in. "It looks nice on you," he commented and then dropped the subject.

Katie smiled to herself. *Score one for Wendy*, she thought. Not that she was going to tell her friend that, at least, not immediately. Wendy was in desperate need of something to occupy her mind and her time. If she thought that her order—it really couldn't be thought of as a suggestion at this point—had borne fruit, there was no telling what her friend might come up with next. Katie *knew* that Wendy was rooting for a torrid romance to ignite between her and Blake, but that just wasn't going to happen. Nobody looking at her, no matter *what* she was wearing, was going to associate the word *torrid* with her name, and she wasn't about to try to recreate herself in some femme fatale role. Blake would probably laugh so hard, he'd wind up injuring himself. Not something she wanted to contemplate.

"So listen," he began, looking, in her opinion, exceedingly uncomfortable. "About yesterday—"

She waited, but his voice had trailed off and he wasn't trying to fill in the void.

"Yes?" she finally asked.

He cleared his throat, intently watching the road. "That was a good idea you had, about dancing. I think that might really impress Brittany."

"That's our main goal," she said brightly, doing her best to keep the note of sarcasm out of her voice. She wasn't quite successful.

"So," he repeated, "I was wondering if you'd mind practicing with me some more—I promise not to let anything get out of hand again." He took a breath, but continued staring straight ahead at the road. "I didn't mean to offend you."

Why in God's name would he think she'd be offended? What was she in his eyes, some Victorian spinster, given to vapors?

"You didn't," she assured him. Then, in case he was going to continue apologizing—something she really didn't want to hear again— she told him, "I've forgotten about it already."

"Oh." He slanted a quick glance at her, then

went back to staring at the emptiness ahead of him. "I guess we're okay then."

"Absolutely." *Just because you're behaving like an idiot, I won't hold it against you*, Katie silently promised.

Blake made an honest, concentrated effort to focus on the steps and techniques Katie was trying to teach him and not on the fact that holding her in his arms caused him to experience a very strong reaction to the woman. Her supple body was at times temptingly brushing against his, at other times pressed so closely to him that the thought of following the dance steps fled completely from his mind.

Those were the times when he would lose his train of thought entirely. His mind a near blank, he would forget to count steps in his head and then stumble, embarrassing himself despite her assurances that this was normal and he was doing fine.

After he stepped on her feet a third time during a rumba, Blake stopped moving altogether and called a halt to the practice. The session, with a few breaks, had gone on for three hours. Enough was enough.

"This just isn't working," he complained.

Unshed tears of pain stung Katie's eyes. This last assault on her feet had almost had her crying out in pain, but she managed to hold it back.

"I tell you what," she suggested with as much cheerfulness as she could muster, "why don't you stick to slow dances for now? You have those mastered—and it doesn't require all that much movement," she pointed out.

He knew what Katie was really saying. "Or stepping on feet."

Katie grinned, her eyes crinkling. "There's that, too."

He supposed he was just frustrated and tired, but there was a small part of him that was wondering why he had never noticed the way her eyes sparkled when she smiled.

Trying to block the thought—and the accompanying sensation that seemed to be shimmying through his system like a random electrical current striking without warning, he asked, "Okay, what's next on the agenda?"

Me, Blake, me. I'm next on the agenda. Or I should be. Brittany's never going to care about you the way that I do.

But there was no point in thinking what she couldn't say out loud, so instead she said, "Next, you're going to write a love letter."

He blinked, staring at her and certain that he couldn't have heard her right. "I'm going to write a what?"

"A love letter," she told him brightly.

Okay, so it wasn't his hearing that was going. It was her mind. "You're kidding, right?"

"No, I'm not kidding." She saw a look that bordered ever so slightly on disgust. Another man who doesn't really like putting his feelings down on paper, she thought. Too bad. "Hey, you're the one who asked me to help you."

Blake had his doubts about the effectiveness of her latest suggestion. "Do women still like things like that?"

"Very much," she told him honestly. *If you wrote "I love you" on the back of a Band-Aid wrapper, I'd keep it forever.*

"But I don't know how to write poetry," he was protesting.

"Who said anything about poetry?" she wanted to know. "A love letter doesn't have to be flowery or rhyme," she assured him. "It just has to be honest. Tell her how you feel."

"I like her. No," he amended, knowing Katie was waiting for more. "I love her."

She kept her smile pasted on her face as she said, "Good start. Now, what else?"

"What else?" he repeated. "There has to be more? What else is there?" he asked, looking as if he was at a complete loss.

Nothing, if you're dealing with a narcissistic Daddy's girl like Brittany. But, for the sake of form, she knew she had to at least go through the motions of helping him, even if her heart was wishing that she would be the one on the receiving end of this yet-to-be-written composition.

"Okay, give me a few minutes," she suggested, sitting down at his desk and kicking off her shoes. "Let me see what I can come up with."

He looked relieved to have her take over. "You're the best, Katie, you know that?"

"I've heard rumors to that effect," she quipped.

Ten minutes later, she looked up from the sheet she was writing on and said, "Okay, this is just a rough draft, but I think this is what you need to tell her." Even as she began to read the love letter out loud, she could feel her own anger begin to rise and fester. In no way did Brittany deserve to receive this.

"Dear Brittany,
I've loved you for a very long time. Whenever I'm not around you, it's as if the sun has left the sky. The only time it comes out again is if I catch a glimpse of you. The sound of your laughter fills my heart with happiness. Whatever went wrong between us the last time is in the past and I would welcome the opportunity to show

*you how much I've grown as a person. I
know that I am now capable of loving you
the way you deserve to be loved."*

Finished, she forced herself to raise her eyes
to his face. "Like I said, it's just a rough draft
right now, but that's the general idea. What do
you think?"

Lost in the words she'd just been reading to
him, it took Blake a moment to extricate himself. Because just for a moment there, watching Katie's lips as she read, he'd felt a glimmer
of something. Something stirring. But then he
roused himself and it was gone.

"What do I think?" he echoed. "I think if
I send that to her, she's absolutely going to
become putty in my hands," he happily responded, all but adding a joyous war whoop
to his words. "You're right, that *is* good. Like
I said, you're just the best, Katie. Send this to
Brittany right away," he instructed.

She hadn't meant to be *that* successful. To
be completely honest, she wasn't striving for
simplicity, she'd been trying for just this side
of nauseating. Obviously, from Blake's enthusiasm, she'd stopped just short of her goal.

Chapter 8

"You look like I feel," Wendy commented when Katie popped her head in later that evening.

Her workday was over and Katie just wanted to make sure that Wendy was all right before she went on to her bedroom and pulled her covers over her head. If she was lucky, she thought dejectedly, she'd suffocate during the night and this nightmare, otherwise known as Project Brittany, would just be a thing of the past.

"Talk to me," Wendy requested with a note of urgency in her voice.

No way was Katie going to unload on Wendy, especially not if she was interpreting

Wendy's demeanor correctly and her friend wasn't feeling well. She wasn't *that* selfish, Katie thought.

Katie flashed a comforting smile at her. "If you're not feeling well, you should rest," Katie told her, then promised, "We'll talk in the morning."

"No, please, talk now," Wendy urged, putting her hand out as if to grasp Katie's—which wasn't exactly possible, given that she was still standing in the bedroom doorway, all the way across the room. "I need some distraction. Juanita just left for the night and Marcos has to stay late because there's a last-minute party booked at Red."

Wendy, ordinarily so full of energy, had to be going out of her mind with boredom, just lying here, day in, day out, Katie thought sympathetically. But there was something in her friend's voice that had her thinking there was another reason for Wendy's need to be distracted that she wasn't telling her.

"Why do you need to be distracted more than usual?" Katie wanted to know.

But Wendy shook her head. She didn't want to talk, didn't want to think.

"No, you first," Wendy insisted. "Why do you look as if you just found out your best friend was sent off to the farm in the country?"

she asked, using the tried-and-true euphemism of parents explaining to their children why a beloved pet could no longer be found roaming around the house.

Katie crossed to the window to the right of Wendy's bed and stared out at the darkness. "You know that Project Brittany that your brother's trying to get off the ground?"

"Yes?"

"Well, I think it's about to take flight." *And I've got no one to blame but myself.*

Wendy filled in the blanks. "No," she protested. "You were supposed to turn the tables on Blake and make him fall in love with you."

Katie leaned her hands on the windowsill. "That was the plan," she agreed and then she sighed. "Unfortunately, I've succeeded *too* well. Blake's sure that he's going to have Brittany eating out of his hand."

"Oh, damn."

Katie smiled sadly at what she assumed was sympathy in her friend's voice. "Yeah, that about sums up the way I feel," she admitted.

"Oh damn, oh damn, *oh damn!*"

Wendy was almost taking this worse than she was, Katie thought. She felt guilty. Wendy had her own set of problems right now.

"It's okay, you don't have to take it that badly. It's not the end of the world, I guess."

She turned from the window to face her friend. "Wendy, I— Oh, God, Wendy, what's wrong?" Katie cried, startled as she took a good look at her best friend.

Wendy's forehead was drenched in sweat and she had all but wadded up her entire blanket beneath her hands. It was as if she was searching for something to anchor her body to the bed, to keep her from spinning out into a world constructed out of an all-consuming, fiery pain.

"Ba-bee," Wendy managed to gasp out between gritted teeth, every inch of her body completely rigid. "The baby's coming!" she screamed.

A cold chill washed over Katie, bringing fear with it. She had to get Wendy to the hospital, but San Antonio Memorial was a good twenty miles away. Wendy didn't look as if she was going to be able to last long enough to get there.

"Hang on, I'm going to get you to the hospital," Katie promised.

She didn't have a car, but she knew that Wendy's was parked in the garage, dormant during her forced encampment. Marcos occasionally used it, just to keep the engine functioning properly, but for the most part, it remained in the garage—which meant that she could drive Wendy to the hospital without any delay.

"C'mon, honey, we're going to get you up," Katie told her.

But as she reached for her, Wendy grabbed her wrist and held it in what could only be termed a vise grip, squeezing it as hard as the contraction was apparently squeezing her.

There was desperation in Wendy's voice when she cried, "No time."

Ordinarily, Katie would have said that Wendy was being dramatic again, but there was something about the look in her eyes that made Katie believe her. She really didn't want to take a chance on being wrong. If that baby was coming, it was better that it come here than in the backseat of a car.

With effort, Katie extricated her wrist from Wendy's death grip. "Okay, we'll stay here." She picked up the cordless receiver from its cradle on the nightstand. "I'll call nine-one-one. They'll send an ambulance—and someone who knows what they're doing."

But Wendy shook her head emphatically. "No...time... Baby...*now*!" she panted, her eyes as huge as saucers.

Because she didn't know what else to do, Katie called anyway.

The maddeningly calm woman on the other

end of the line asked the nature of the emergency and then wanted details. As coherently as possible, given that her heart was now lodged in her throat, Katie rattled off the problem and Wendy's address. She ended with a request for an ambulance. NOW.

"And a doctor," she added almost as an afterthought. "I need a doctor on the line," she cried just as Wendy scrunched up her face again.

"I'm afraid we don't have a doctor here," the dispatcher told her.

"Call…my…doctor," Wendy gasped, curling up into a ball and rocking back and forth, "…press three…speed…dial."

Katie immediately disconnected her call and then followed Wendy's instruction, praying that the dispatcher she'd talked to would come through with that ambulance she'd requested.

The doctor wasn't in, but given the hour, that was to be expected. Katie prayed she could track him down in time.

"The doctor is making his rounds at the hospital," the woman at the answering service informed her routinely. "Dr. Nickelson will be back in his office tomorrow morning at—"

Grasping the receiver with both hands, Katie said in a barely controlled, desperate voice, "Now, you listen to me. Tomorrow morning's too late. This baby is coming *now* and it's just Wendy and me here. You patch me through to Dr. Nickelson this minute. I need him to talk me through the delivery or God only knows what's going to happen. Do you understand me?" she demanded.

"I understand," the woman replied, suddenly sounding very human and sympathetic. "Hold on, I'm going to patch you through. Don't hang up."

"Not on your life," Katie said, but she was talking to a temporarily dead phone. Wendy cried out in pain. She squeezed Wendy's shoulder, feeling incredibly helpless. Praying that the answering service could get ahold of the doctor. "Hang on, Wendy, I'm getting help."

Five seconds later, the line came back to life and a deep baritone said, "This is Dr. Nickelson," into her ear. Before she could begin to give the physician a summary of what was going on, Wendy screamed again. That took care of any necessary introduction. "How far along is she?" Dr. Nickelson asked.

"Passed the goal line," Katie answered, as she looked at Wendy's contorted face.

Because he needed something concrete, Dr. Nickelson restated his question. "How far is she dilated?"

Oh God. "Sorry," Katie murmured to Wendy

as she threw back the covers with one hand and then pulled up her friend's nightgown.

"Just…get…it…out!" Wendy pleaded, tears she wasn't even away of streaming down her face.

Katie's heart was hammering so hard, she could barely draw a breath. "I can see the head." Crowning, that was called crowning, she suddenly remembered. "She's crowning."

"Put the phone on speaker," the doctor told her, his voice calm, soothing. "You're going to need two hands. Is Wendy lying down in bed?"

What did that have to do with anything? she thought impatiently. "Yes," Katie all but snapped.

"Good. You need to get her propped up against the headboard so she has something to lean against as she pushes."

As quickly and gently as possible, Katie pulled Wendy up in bed so that her shoulders were up against the headboard.

"Done," she called out.

"Good," the deep voice pronounced again. "Now position yourself on the receiving end," he instructed as if this was an everyday oc-curence. "On the count of three, I want you to have her bear down and push as hard as she can. One—two—"

"THREE!" Wendy shrieked, then bore down

for all she was worth, desperately trying to expel the baby and the pain at the same time. All she managed to expel was a gutteral sound that didn't sound quite human.

"Now stop," the disembodied voice on the speakerphone ordered.

"I…can't…do…this!" Wendy sobbed.

"Yes, you can and you will," Katie fired back in a no-nonsense voice, sensing that if she gave Wendy sympathy, her friend would really fall apart. She prayed that she wasn't in over her head. Over *both* their heads, she amended.

Blake took out the key that Wendy had given him and inserted it into the lock. He'd already swung by once this evening, but that was to drop Katie off. For once, he hadn't gone in and it was guilt that had brought him back. After all, his initial reason for being out here in the first place was because Wendy was a prisoner in her own bedroom until the baby made his or her appearance in the world. To allow himself to get so caught up in his pursuit of Brittany that he forgot to spend a little time with Wendy was just plain wrong.

Granted Katie was here with her, but it was Wendy he was really here to see, he told himself.

He stopped dead a second after he closed the

front door. And then, just like that, he heard a baby cry. He ran up the stairs and heard Katie's voice coming from the bedroom. He burst in and was amazed—and surprisingly, nearly overcome with emotion—at the sight before him.

"It's here!" Katie announced, feeling her own body shaking as she held this brand-new tiny damp life between her hands. "You have a girl, Wendy," she nearly sobbed. "You have a girl." Her own head spinning badly and it took effort for her to concentrate. There was still a lot more she had to do, but for the life of her, Katie couldn't think of what that was.

At that moment the doorbell rang. "It must be the paramedics."

Blake turned to her and said, "You've done more than enough tonight. I'll go downstairs and let them in. You stay here." As he crossed to the doorway, he paused for a moment and looked at her over his shoulder. "You were magnificent," he told her in a voice filled with admiration.

His warm smile embedded itself under her skin even before he left the room.

Chapter 9

When she looked back on all this later, Katie hadn't really intended to go to the hospital with Wendy and the baby, especially not in the back of the ambulance. Now that the baby had been safely delivered, she just wanted to get out of the paramedics' way and let them see to Wendy and her tiny girl. After all, the EMTs were the professionals and would take good care of both of them.

But one look at her best friend's eyes was all it had taken. It told Katie that Wendy, despite her bravado, was still shaken, still in need of reassurance. Still in need of a familiar face to be there with her.

So, at the last minute, she suddenly heard herself calling out, "Wait up. I'm going with her."

The paramedic inside the back of the ambulance looked a little dubious for a second, then nodded. "Okay, come on," he said as he extended his hand to her.

Grasping it, she got on and then perched on the tiny bit of space beside Wendy's gurney. She had no idea how she was going to get back to Red Rock and the house, but that didn't matter right now. All that mattered was that her best friend still needed her—at least until Marcos could be reached so that he could come down to the hospital to be with his wife.

"She's so tiny," Wendy murmured, exhaustion and a mother's concern evident in every syllable. "Do you think she'll be all right?"

"She's a survivor," Katie assured her. "And look who her mother is. Of course she'll be all right."

Wendy looked up at her. "Thank you."

"Just telling you the truth," Katie replied, shrugging off the thanks.

"No, I mean for everything. For being there and bringing the baby into the world."

Katie smiled warmly. "She brought herself into the world. I was just the cheering section," she said, looking at the very tiny bundle for the moment sleeping against Wendy's breast.

Kissing the top of her baby's head, Wendy looked back at Katie. There was wonder and disbelief mingled in her eyes.

"I'm a mother, Katie," she said in hushed awe.

Katie smiled. "I know. I was there."

When the ambulance finally arrived at San Antonio Memorial's E.R. entrance, a team of nurses and a doctor were waiting for them. Mother and baby were whisked off to the recovery area, where they were separated and taken in different directions. Since the newest member of the Mendoza/Fortune family was on the rather small side, the physician on duty felt it best to place the infant in an incubator, at least to begin with. Wendy looked stricken when the baby was taken from her arms, but she knew it was for the best.

Just like that, Katie found herself standing alone outside the recovery room doors, relegated to the hallway. Having nowhere else to be, unfamiliar with the hospital layout and too tired to go exploring at this hour, she resigned herself to remaining where she was until such time as Wendy was taken up to a room on the maternity floor.

With a sigh, Katie leaned against the wall and closed her eyes. She hadn't realized just how very tired and drained she was until this very minute. She wondered if anyone would say anything if she just stretched out on the floor, out of the way. Things were relatively quiet and at a lull right now. Her mind began to drift, floating to different levels as sleep began to creep in around her, taking more and more of her away.

Someone placed a hand on her shoulder. "Is she inside there?"

Katie's eyes flew open. At the same time, she stifled a surprised gasp. The hand on her shoulder belonged to Blake. She hadn't expected him to come. He hadn't said anything about following her to the hospital. "What are you doing here?" she asked him.

Blake was by turns surprised and then amused by her question. "She's my sister, remember? And besides, I thought you might like a ride home—unless you've already made other plans," he qualified.

But Katie shook her head. "No, no plans," she admitted. "After what just happened, I'm afraid I haven't thought that far ahead."

Blake looked genuinely stunned. "Wow, Katie Wallace without a plan. This really is a red-letter day, isn't it?"

She took a deep breath, doing what she could to pull herself together.

"You might say that." There was something she needed to ask him—oh, right. Marcos. She turned to Blake and asked, "Did you call Marcos?"

He nodded. "The minute you took off in the ambulance with Wendy and the baby. He's on his way. I offered to pick him up, but he said he wasn't about to wait. I think he started running to the car the second he heard my voice." The bemused smile on his lips was mixed with concern as Blake shook his head. "I sure hope the roads are clear tonight. This would be a hell of a bad time for him to get into an accident."

Maybe it was because she was punchy, but the wording he'd just used amused her. "And exactly when is a good time?"

Blake stared at her, confused. He was beginning to feel that confusion was a somewhat regular occurrence around Katie these days. She said things that scrambled his brain lately—especially since he'd kissed her.

"What?"

"To get into an accident. You said now's a bad time for him to get into an accident and I'm asking if there's a good time to get into one?" she asked innocuously.

Definitely out to scramble his brain, he decided. "Point taken."

When he continued just standing in the hallway with her, saying nothing further, she felt compelled to ask, "Shouldn't you be calling your family?"

To be honest, Blake had felt so blown away by having taken an active part in the miracle of birth, calling everyone had completely slipped his mind. Trust Katie to remember, he thought. The woman really was very good at details.

"What would I do without you?" he asked, shaking his head as he took out his cell phone.

"Start keeping track of your own calendar, comes to mind," she quipped. Although it was exceedingly tempting, she refused to allow herself to take to heart too much of what he had just said. He hadn't meant anything by it. Probably didn't even know he'd said it, she thought, ruefully.

"You do it better," he told her seriously. Moving away from Katie for the sake of privacy, he pressed the first programmed number on his cell.

Instead of making five separate calls, Blake decided to just call his sister, Emily.

"Hello?" a sleepy voice said after the fourth ring.

He'd forgotten about the time difference. "Emily, it's Blake. I'm sorry, I didn't mean to wake you. This damn time difference tripped me up," he apologized.

Hearing her brother's voice, the woman on the other end of the line became instantly alert. "What's wrong? Why are you calling?"

"Just thought you might want to know that you're officially an aunt now. Wendy had her baby about an hour ago." This uncle business was going to take some getting used to.

"Tell me everything. What does she weigh? How big is she?" Emily asked, eager for details.

He couldn't elaborate on any of that, he realized ruefully. "That's all I know right now. Wendy had the baby at home. Katie delivered it."

Emily was immediately concerned. "Oh my God—is Wendy all right?"

"Wendy's fine," he assured her. "She and the baby are at the hospital now. I'll call when I know more—but until then, could you do me a favor? Could you call Mom and Dad and the others and tell them?"

"Sure, no problem," Emily marveled, her voice growing soft. "I can't wait to see her. Give Wendy a hug for me and tell her I'll be there as soon as I can." And with that, Emily terminated the call so that she could call everyone else in the family and alert them to this latest development: the Fortunes of Atlanta had a granddaughter.

Blake closed his phone and put it away. He felt his energy dissipating and decided he needed an infusion of coffee—decent if possible, but at least black if the former was too much to ask for.

As it turned out, he had to settle for vending-machine coffee, which by definition was mediocre. He brought back two cups, one black and one so light it looked more like white-chocolate milk than coffee.

Katie was exactly where he'd left her, holding up the wall with her back and appearing as if she was about to drift off to sleep that way.

"Sugar and a ton of cream, right?" he asked as he handed her the appropriate paper cup.

That was enough to banish her fatigue, at least for the time being. "You remembered," she said in surprise.

To her recollection, Blake had never gotten her coffee. If anything, it had been the other way around, not that she minded. She had never felt it necessary to define herself by what she did or didn't do. Besides, if she was willing to groom Blake so that he would be more appealing to Brittany, bringing an occasional cup of coffee to the man was no big deal.

Having him bring coffee to her, however, was a big deal. At least in her book.

"I pay attention," Blake protested, then amended, "Sometimes," when Katie gave him a penetrating, knowing look.

Her smile was warm and grateful. "Thank you." She peeled off the plastic lid and then took a long, appreciative sip. "I really need this," she told him as she felt the warm liquid wind its way through her sleepy system. "I'm dead on my feet."

His eyes casually swept over her. For a wilting flower, she looked damn good. Maybe too good, he judged a split second before he banked down his thoughts. It was just the exhaustion taking over, he told himself, taking him to places he didn't intend to go.

"Could have fooled me," he commented. And then, changing the subject, he looked up and down the hallway. No one was coming. "Any word from Marcos?"

The question had no sooner left his lips than Marcos turned a corner and came barreling down the hallway, looking like a man who had run rather than driven the twenty miles to the hospital from the Red Rock restaurant he managed.

"Where is she?" he cried, latching onto his brother-in-law's arm. "Where's Wendy?"

"Catch your breath, Marcos," Katie told him. "Wendy's still in recovery."

Alarmed, his system on overload, Marcos cried, "Why? What's she doing there?"

"Recovering," Katie answered simply. "It was a big ordeal, Marcos," she elaborated, then couldn't help adding, "for all concerned. Her doctor wants to be perfectly sure she's all right before he sends Wendy to her room."

The fact that Katie had mentioned only his wife suddenly registered. "And the baby?" he asked suddenly. "Where's Mary Anne?"

"She's in an incubator. She's fine," Katie told him quickly when his worried expression only deepened, all but pinching his handsome features. "She's just a little small right now, but the doctor said that was to be expected, remember?" Katie placed her hand on Marcos's shoulder. "She looks perfect," Katie assured him. "Trust me."

She wasn't prepared for what happened next. One moment, she was talking to Wendy's distraught husband, trying to reassure him, the next moment Marcos was suddenly enveloping her in what could only be described as a bear hug.

Caught off guard, Katie could only stand there, stunned and motionless for a moment, her arms pinned to her sides.

"Marcos?" she asked uncertainly. "Are *you* all right?"

"Blake told me everything you did, delivering the baby and keeping Wendy calm. I don't know if she would have made it without you. Thank you," he cried, squeezing her hard again. "Thank you!"

The more he thanked her, the harder he squeezed, until she couldn't draw any air in. "No need to thank me," she all but squeaked. The next moment, he released her and it was hard not to just go limp, but she managed to hold herself together. She gulped in a lungful of air. "I'm just glad I was there and could help. It's a pretty humbling experience," she confessed.

If either Marcos or Blake were going to say anything, she never got the chance to hear it because, just then, the double doors leading into the recovery room swung open. A nurse came out, guiding the foot of a gurney while an orderly pushed it out of the room and toward the service elevator.

Marcos instinctively moved out of the way before he realized that his wife was the patient on the gurney. When he did, his face lit up like a Fourth of July sparkler.

"Wendy," he cried, taking her hand in his and walking quickly beside the moving gurney. "I'm sorry I wasn't there. If I'd had the slightest idea that you were going to—"

"I'm not sorry," Wendy said truthfully, cutting into his apology. She saw no reason for it. "I wasn't exactly at my best."

"You were having our baby." Marcos's eyes were filled with love as he looked at his wife. "I can't think of a time when you could have looked more beautiful to me," he told her honestly.

Following behind the gurney, Katie deliberately fell back and then stopped walking altogether. Wendy and her husband needed some time alone together.

"Now, there's a marriage that's going to last forever," she murmured in admiration and envy.

"Think so?" Blake asked.

She hadn't realized she'd said the words out loud, or that Blake was so close to her. She flushed, embarrassed, but there was no pretending she'd meant something else—or that she wasn't just a tiny bit envious.

"Yes, I do," she said with conviction. "Marcos knows exactly what to say to make her feel beautiful, even when she knows, deep down, that appearance-wise, she's had better days."

He nodded, as if her words made perfect sense. This really *was* a red-letter day, she couldn't help thinking. Either that, or she'd fallen asleep against the recovery room wall and this was all a dream.

"Are you ready to go home," Blake asked, "or do you want to go upstairs to her room?"

Despite the coffee, she was having trouble battling exhaustion, which had returned stronger than ever and seemed only a half step or so away from flattening her. "Oh, so ready," she confessed.

Blake nodded with a smile, ready to turn in himself. "Home it is."

Katie fell asleep almost the moment he pulled out of the space in the hospital parking lot. She was still asleep when they reached the house, some twenty-five miles later. Pulling up the hand brake and turning off the engine, Blake looked at his sleeping passenger. He debated waking her, then thought better of it.

Instead, he got out of the vehicle and went to the front door. He unlocked it with the key that Wendy had given him. Then, leaving the door open, he returned to his car and opened the passenger-side door.

Her face looked softer when she was asleep, he thought. More at ease. He wasn't certain just how long he stood there, looking at her, letting his thoughts drift, before he snapped back to attention. He was grateful there was no one around to witness it.

Taking a breath, he very gently eased Katie out of the car and into his arms. She hardly weighed anything, he thought as he turned toward the house. Like a bridegroom with his new bride, he carried Katie across the threshold and then proceeded to carry her up the stairs.

She made a slight, dreamy noise just as he came to the landing and that in turn woke her up. A contented sigh escaped her before she opened her eyes.

As her surroundings penetrated, her eyes widened proportionately. By then she was inside her room. The next moment, she felt herself being lowered to her bed. She looked up uncertainly at the man who had brought her here.

"Blake?"

Anticipating her question, Blake explained, "You fell asleep. I didn't have the heart to wake you, and leaving you sleeping in the car didn't seem like a good option, either."

"So you carried me into the house?" she marveled. Who did that these days? That was straight out of some period piece—and she loved it!

Blake shrugged dismissively. "Seemed like the right thing to do at the time."

"I'm sorry," she apologized, feeling a tad self-conscious. "You should have woken me up."

He laughed softly. "Where's the chivalry in that?" he wanted to know.

"I don't know about chivalry, but at least your back wouldn't hurt." If he'd hurt it because of her, she'd never forgive herself....

"My back's fine. You don't even weigh as much as a sack of flour," he told her.

"I've had more flattering comparisons," she told him with a self-deprecating laugh.

"I'm sure you have," he agreed. "But none more sincere," he guaranteed. When she began to get up, he said, "Stay in bed, Katie."

"Is that an order?" she asked whimsically. *Or an invitation?* she added both silently and wistfully.

"It is if you need it to be," he told her. "Do you?" And then he smiled to himself. He was talking to an unconscious woman. Katie had fallen asleep again. Had to have been a hell of a day for her, he thought. He knew it had been for him.

Funny, he would have sworn that he knew Katie's limitations, having grown up with her. And yet, she had surprised him today, both with the way she had taken charge when his sister had gone into labor, and with her resilience and determination to be there for Wendy until Marcos arrived. And then, even though she looked utterly wiped out, she was the one who'd recalled that his family needed to be notified when he clearly should have been the one to remember.

Which just told him that, no matter how well you thought you knew someone, there were still surprises in the offing.

He paused long enough to lightly drape the end of her comforter over Katie and brush back the hair that had fallen into her face.

She looked peaceful, he thought. God only knew she'd earned it.

He'd let her sleep in tomorrow, he decided. There was no need to get started at the crack of dawn. Nine o'clock or so would be early enough. He had a feeling that tomorrow would be, in large measure, taken up by visits to Wendy and Mary Anne.

That was okay, he thought with affection. There was no hurry to get on with Project Brittany. As far as he was concerned they were already ahead of schedule. Besides, even if they weren't, Brittany wasn't going anywhere. The Valentine's Day fund-raiser where he intended to make his move was more than a week away.

Brittany had already agreed to go with him. Not because of any resurging affection on her part—she had a very practical reason for attending it with him.

He wasn't about to fool himself. She was in need of an escort and he had been in the right place at the right time. She wouldn't miss the annual event for the world. A great many people would be attending and she liked—no, loved—making an entrance, he thought.

As a matter of fact, she never missed an opportunity to be seen and fawned over. She was like an exquisite work of art and exquisite works of art, needed an audience to be properly viewed and admired, he thought. It was probably one of the first lessons that Brittany had ever learned. That, and that turning heads was extremely good for the ego.

And God knew that Brittany had no problem in that department, he mused. Her ego was alive and thriving.

Unlike Katie, he caught himself thinking.

Glancing at her one last time, Blake shut the light and eased her bedroom door closed. He deliberately ignored the odd, unsettled feeling in the pit of his stomach, the one that seemed to hint that the girl he'd grown up next to had turned in to the kind of woman he could grow old with.

Chapter 10

The dream was so vivid, so moving, Katie felt it with every fiber of her being. Her body heated as the seconds ticked by, bringing with them more and more pieces to fill her mind.

But even while it was unfolding, she knew it *had* to be a dream. Because Blake was paying attention to *her*. Right in the middle of writing a love letter to Brittany—a sizzling, *hot* love letter, Blake had used her name rather than Brittany's. When she'd pointed out his mistake, he'd looked into her eyes and told her that for the first time in his life, he wasn't making a mistake. That his initial belief that he was in love with Brittany had been the real mistake.

And then he'd taken her into his arms and,

suddenly they were dancing—and then they weren't. Because he was kissing her. Caressing her. Making love to her with every breath he took.

Katie couldn't remember when she'd been happier.

And then daylight had crept into her consciousness, nudging her awake, banishing sleep. She screwed her eyes up tight, reluctant to leave this make-believe place her mind had created for her.

But it was no use.

The dream broke up into wisps of vapor and then was gone.

With a sigh, she gave up and got out of bed. A quick shower had her almost feeling human. She had made her way down the stairs and reached the kitchen when the silence finally penetrated. She was alone in the house. Marcos, she realized, must have remained in the hospital with Wendy. Which was where Katie wanted to be.

The problem was how to get there.

Her first impulse was to call the man who had been her mode of transportation ever since she'd arrived in Red Rock. But her call to Blake's cell phone went straight to voice mail. Katie was in no mood to leave a message that Blake would listen to God only knew when.

She terminated the call abruptly, muttering a few choice words under her breath.

Frustrated and antsy, Katie impulsively went into the garage to see if there were any vehicles available. Marcos's sedan was gone, just as she knew it would be, but Wendy's car—the one Wendy had offered to let her drive on more than one occasion since she'd arrived here— was still there.

A peek inside told her the vehicle was all gassed up and ready to go.

She'd initially turned Wendy's offer down because she didn't like being responsible for someone else's car. They were called *accidents* for a reason—but this fell under the heading of an emergency, or at least something close to it, she reasoned.

The debate in her head went on for all of two minutes before it tilted toward yes. She retraced her steps back to the kitchen. As she recalled, Wendy kept her car keys hanging on a peg next to the bay window over the sink.

They were still there.

Ten minutes later Katie found herself hitting the open road. She was on her way to San Antonio and the hospital, thanks to the GPS device perched on the dashboard.

She left Wendy's vehicle in the hospital's guest parking lot, silently counting the number of cars in her row, and hurried into the hospital.

Her first order of business, Katie decided happily as she got into the elevator car, was to look in on the tiny human being she'd helped bring into the world last night. The infant wasn't even a day old yet, Katie thought with a wide grin as she got off on the maternity floor.

She'd never known anyone that young before.

Turning a corner, Katie stopped and hesitated for a moment. She debated quietly slipping away until Marcos was finished visiting with his daughter. He was looking at the infant through the glass.

The tiny girl looked even smaller in the incubator, Katie decided.

The deeply concerned look on Marcos's face made Katie's mind up for her. She not only stayed but came forward and made herself known to him.

"She's doing fine, Marcos," Katie assured him, even as she placed a comforting hand on the man's shoulder.

Lost in thought as he stared at his daughter, Marcos jumped, startled, and swung around to see who was talking to him.

When he saw that it was Katie, he relaxed. "Oh, it's you."

Katie took a step back, not wanting to crowd him. "I'm sorry, I didn't mean to catch you off guard like that."

He waved away her apology. "I should be the one who's saying he's sorry. I was preoccupied," he explained. "I didn't even hear you come up."

His preoccupation brought her full circle, back to the concerned look she'd seen on his face. "You don't have to worry. The doctor told me she was very healthy," Katie said, in case he didn't recall her having said that to him last night.

Marcos nodded, a weary smile half curving his mouth. "I know. It's not her I'm worried about."

Katie jumped to the only conclusion she could. If he wasn't worried about the baby, that could only mean one thing. "Did something happen to Wendy—?" Even as she asked, she half turned, ready to dash down the hall to Wendy's room.

He was quick to shoot down her mistake. "No, Wendy, thanks to you, is doing just great." And for that she had his undying gratitude. "I'm just worried about Javier," he confessed. Backtracking, Marcos explained, "I spent the night here, in Wendy's room—one of the orderlies brought a cot in for me," he told her. "This morning I went to look in on Javier, to give him the good news about the baby being born. He congratulated me and said to give his love to Wendy, but I could see that he was still having a really hard time dealing with his injuries. He'd always been so damn healthy, he doesn't know how to handle this."

Filled with frustrated energy and no release, Marcos fought the urge to start pacing. That wouldn't do any good. The only thing that might help would be to knocking some sense into Javier's head—literally.

"I know he thinks he's never going to walk again and in his mind, that makes him half a man. It's insane to think that way, but to be honest," he told Katie, dropping his voice, "if I were in Javier's place, I don't know if I'd be thinking any differently."

Katie took Marcos's hand, as if to somehow physically transfer her own feelings to him. "He *is* going to walk again, Marcos. He really has to believe that," she insisted. And then she looked at him for a long moment. "You have to *make* him believe that. A positive attitude is really important in this kind of a case. And besides," she said, never wavering, "miracles happen every day, so why not for Javier?"

Marcos searched her eyes and realized that his wife's friend wasn't just saying something to make him feel better. "You honestly believe that, don't you?"

Katie nodded with conviction. "From the bottom of my heart."

Right now, he was willing to cling to anything, as long as it helped Javier get back on his feet. "I suppose, maybe miracles do happen," Marcos said, his tone just a wee bit guarded. "If you hadn't been there for Wendy and the baby last night, I might have lost them both."

She didn't like to dwell on that. Negatives were things she preferred to banish from her thoughts. "Instead, they're happy and healthy," she said cheerfully. "If you'd like me to, I could go and talk to Javier, make him see that there's every reason in the world to believe that he's going to get better. All it takes is patience and time—" she offered.

Touched, Marcos kissed her cheek. "No, you've already done more than enough for the Mendoza family," he told her, emotion brimming in his voice. "Dealing with my brother is my job. Tell you what. Why don't you head on to Wendy's room? I know she's dying to see you. You should go now, before everyone else gets here and it gets too noisy and too crowded."

"Crowded?" she repeated, a little confused.

He nodded. "Last I heard, they were all getting ready to fly back out here. Together." He liked Wendy's family, but if he were honest, he preferred them in small doses. This did not promise to be a small dose. "It's going to be standing room only around her bed."

"By everyone, you mean her brothers and sisters, right?" she asked cautiously. She knew what Wendy's father was like and it had been difficult tearing the man away from his desk long enough to attend the wedding.

"And her parents," Marcos added.

Katie made no attempt to hide her surprise. "You're kidding. Her father's coming?"

She would have expected Wendy's mother to want to come, but the woman rarely did anything on her own and her husband was all but married to his job. In her opinion, the foundation was his real wife and Wendy's mother was more like the mistress he had on the side.

Marcos laughed shortly, glad he wasn't the only one who felt that way.

"Surprised me, too. John Michael Fortune leaving his office twice in the space of a little over a month—I expected the Second Coming to happen before that. Just goes to show you, you really can never tell the kind of power a newborn baby has," he said with a laugh.

Marcos looked a lot better now than he had when she had first seen him in the hallway,

Katie thought, a sense of satisfaction sweeping through her. Her work here was done.

"Then I'd better go see Wendy quickly," she agreed, starting to leave.

Marcos nodded, turning back to the nursery window. "Tell her I'll be along after I finish visiting with my daughter."

"I'll tell her."

That really was one lucky little girl. Marcos was going to make a great father, Katie thought.

She smiled to herself as she went down the hallway, reading off the room numbers until she came to Wendy's. She knocked on the closed door. But rather than stand on ceremony, waiting for a verbal invitation to come in, Katie pushed open the door and went in. After last night, she and Wendy had crossed a new threshold. The intensity of their relationship had deepened by several remarkable layers.

Wendy looked really pleased to see her. Blake, who was also in the room, was the one who was surprised.

"I thought after last night, you'd be sleeping in, recharging your batteries, that kind of thing," he told her.

The dream still very fresh in her mind, her pulse launched into double time at the very sight of Blake. Katie fervently hoped that a flush hadn't crept into her face, giving her away.

She did her best to focus on the present—and reality—not a wishful dream that hadn't a chance in hell of coming true.

"I don't need much sleep," Katie informed him almost stiffly. After all, he'd been through the same thing she had and now here he was, bright-eyed and bushy-tailed. Why did he think she would be anything less than that? Did he think of her as some fragile cream puff? "I helped Wendy deliver a baby, I didn't carve out the Grand Canyon with a soup spoon," she pointed out crisply.

Blake shrugged. Men were supposed to be heartier than women, but he knew better than to say that out loud. Besides, it was apparent that Katie was every bit as hearty as he was.

And then something occurred to him.

"Hold it. Since I pick you up every day and I'm here, just how did you get to the hospital?" Katie was extremely levelheaded and practically frugality personified. He couldn't see her calling a taxi to bring her here. So then, how had she gotten here? There was no public transportation that would have brought her from Red Rock.

"Magic," she retorted, remaining mysterious

for exactly half a second before she confessed to Wendy. "I borrowed your car. You did tell me I could use it," she reminded her friend, mentally crossing her fingers and hoping that it was still all right.

Wendy put her hand on top of Katie's and smiled warmly. "After what you did last night, everything I have is yours," she said with feeling.

Relieved, Katie laughed. "Marcos might have a different opinion about that. Borrowing your car to come see you is all the payment I want," she told Wendy.

"Well, I'll leave you two alone to talk," Blake told his sister. "I'm going to go take another look at my niece and then head back to Red Rock."

"But you'll be back later this evening?" Wendy asked hopefully.

Blake knew exactly what his sister was really asking. "You mean when the Fortune family descends en masse? Sure, I'll be here. Wouldn't miss seeing the expression on the old man's face when he looks at his granddaughter for the first time." Although, he thought, his father would have undoubtedly been happier if the first grandchild had been a boy, born to one of his sons. "He's probably bringing a tiny little desk and chair for her so she can get started working for the company by the time she learns how to sit up." He lapsed into a deep voice, doing a fair imitation of their father. "'No time like the present, Wendy. You're never too young to start on the right path.'"

"Your father's not as bad as all that," Katie protested, coming to the man's defense. When her own late father had faced ruin, it was the senior Fortune who had found a position for him in his own company. She would always be grateful to him for allowing her father the chance to restore his dignity and his pride.

"Oh, yes, he is," Wendy and Blake told her in unison.

Not wanting to argue with her friends, Katie relented. It still didn't change the truth, in her eyes. She knew that John Michael had a great deal of difficulty in expressing his feelings, but in that he was not unlike a lot of other men, especially those in his generation. The bottom line was that he was coming, and that meant a great deal.

With a shrug, Katie retreated, saying, "Can't argue with both of you."

The look Blake gave her sent a shiver up her spine that she had a great deal of difficulty in masking. "Sure you can," he quipped as he went out the door. "And probably will."

Wendy pushed a button and the top portion

of her mattress pivoted forward, allowing her to almost sit up. "So," she asked eagerly the second Blake had closed the door behind him, "how's it going?"

For a split second, Katie had let her mind stray back to her dream. She shook herself free when she heard Wendy's voice and looked at her friend. "What?"

Wendy rolled her eyes. "This so-called Project Brittany of his."

Katie was surprised that Wendy even wanted to talk about that, given the little miracle lying in the incubator down the hall. But her friend was looking at her eagerly, obviously waiting for some sort of a progress report.

She shrugged. "I was going to show him how to cook today, but I'm not sure if that's still on, given the circumstances." She looked at Wendy pointedly.

"Circumstances?" Wendy echoed.

How could Wendy even ask? "You, the baby—ring a bell?" Katie asked, her eyes meeting Wendy's. How could she even *think* of anything else? If she'd just had a baby…but then, that was never going to happen to her. She was probably just going to be "fun Aunt Katie" and wind up dying alone, while eating her dinner standing over her kitchen sink.

She didn't expect Wendy to become indignant and raise her voice. "Don't you dare stop because of me. I want you there, shoulder to shoulder with Blake until my empty-headed brother realizes that you are three times the woman that Brittany will *ever* be."

Katie shook her head. Maybe this was just a futile battle and she was fooling herself that she could get Blake to see the light.

"I don't know about that, Wendy," she confessed honestly. "Brittany's a socialite, she moves in your circle."

Wendy instantly came to her defense. "And you are a real person who doesn't *need* a circle. Now, please," she entreated, "if you're not going to do this for yourself, do it for Blake."

Katie frowned. Had the delivery wiped out Wendy's short-term memory? "Blake wants Brittany, remember?" she said with a note of dejection.

"No, my brother only *thinks* he wants Brittany," Wendy corrected. "And if by some horrible prank of nature, he managed to temporarily—and I stress the word *temporarily*—get her, what he'd wind up getting is cotton candy."

"Cotton candy?" Katie repeated. Just what was that supposed to mean?

Wendy nodded her head. "No substance, just air and sugar. And she'll break his heart on top of that," Wendy predicted. "She did it once, she'll do it again. That's one leopard who is *not* changing her shallow spots." She moved closer to Katie, taking her hand and saying earnestly, "Trust me, my brother needs a good woman in his life—and as far as I can see, there's only one good woman in this mix and it's you, Katie." She sighed, suddenly feeling exhausted. Leaning back on her pillows, Wendy released Katie's hand. "So go, get back to Scott's and get back to work. Save my stupid brother from himself and the stupidest mistake he could ever possibly make." Her eyes narrowed. "Kill her if you have to. You have my permission."

The atmosphere had been deadly serious—until the last two sentences. The tension dissipated and Katie laughed, shaking her head.

"Don't be shy, Wendy," she said in a coaxing tone. "Tell me what you really think."

"Go!" Wendy repeated, a slight grin on her lips as she pointed toward the door.

Katie saluted as if she were a dutiful little soldier. "Okay."

"And don't forget to call me and tell me how it's going," Wendy added, raising her voice as she called after her departing friend.

"Will do," Katie promised, just as the door closed behind her. "Provided there's something worth reporting," she added under her breath.

* * *

Blake looked up in surprise from the desk where he was making notes to himself. He hadn't heard her knock—she probably hadn't, he decided—but he had sensed rather than heard her the second she'd entered the make-shift office. It was, he thought, as if he'd somehow gotten attuned to Katie.

But then, why not? They'd worked together for over two years now, hadn't they? You got used to a person's habits and the scent they wore after two years, he reasoned. Provided, of course, that they wore a scent, he added wryly.

Out loud, to cover his surprise, he said, "I didn't expect to see you here today."

Katie put her purse down. "Why not? It's another 'work' day, right? Since you're here, you obviously didn't take it off," she pointed out. *You're that eager to win the wrong girl*, she added silently while maintaining a smile on her lips.

Blake nodded at the paper on his desk. "I thought I'd polish up that love letter you wrote for me. You know, add my own touches to it." He looked at her with just a little bit of hesitation. Or was he being thoughtful of her feelings? She caught herself wondering before dismissing the thought as merely wishful thinking. "You don't mind, do you?"

She shrugged. "It's your love letter." God, had that sounded as awkward to him as it did to her?

To her surprise, he pushed the letter aside. "I can work on that later. So, you have anything new in mind?" he asked her, sounding every bit like an eager student.

Oh, God, this man is so wasted on Brittany, she thought in despair. "I thought today I'd teach you how to cook."

"Cook?" he repeated, then frowned. Deeply. "Is that really necessary? I mean, isn't the saying, 'The way to a man's heart is through his stomach,' pretty clear that it's the woman who does the cooking? Not that I think that Brittany could boil an egg," he confessed.

She'd probably set the house on fire if she tried, Katie thought. "That saying was popular when women were regarded as second-class citizens. Times have changed," she reminded him. "Now, if you don't think you're up to it…" She let her voice trail off.

Nothing got him more motivated than a challenge. "Bring it," he said.

Katie nodded her head with a smile. *I fully intend to, Blake. I fully intend to.*

Chapter 11

"No, no, you *stir* the flour slowly into the consommé, you don't beat it as if you're some outraged supermodel, out for revenge," Katie protested.

On her way over to Scott Fortune's house, she had stopped at the store to pick up a few ingredients for the proposed cooking lesson. She'd decided to get Blake started by having him prepare beef Stroganoff, thinking it was a relatively easy recipe.

Apparently she'd thought wrong.

One second, she'd turned away for *one* second to retrieve the mushrooms from the refrigerator and when she'd turned back again, it was to see Blake all but attacking the pot, which now contained the carefully diced-up beef, the consommé and supposedly the evenly distributed quarter cup of flour.

"But it's all lumpy," Blake complained in frustration. He was unsuccessfully trying to change the consistency of the flour—which was beginning to look like dumplings at this stage—by hitting each small lump with the flat of his spatula. "It's not supposed to be lumpy, right?"

She suppressed the desire to laugh and solemnly said, "Right."

That could have been avoided if he'd poured the flour in slowly, stirring as he went, the way she'd told him to. But he had obviously just up-ended the measuring cup and tossed all four ounces in at once. Still, there was no point in mentioning that to him now. Now was the time for damage control.

"You *stir* like this," Katie told him, covering his hand with her own and moving the large spatula rhythmically inside the pot. "Get the feel of it?" she asked.

He turned his head, looking back over his shoulder at her. She was directly behind him, less than a hair's breadth away.

As close as the next heartbeat, he realized. "Yeah, I feel it," he murmured.

His breath seemed to graze her skin. Or was

that just the steam coming up from the Stroganoff? The spatula in the pot wasn't the only thing being stirred, Katie couldn't help thinking. Belatedly, she released his hand and drew her own away.

Getting her heartbeat regulated took another minute or so longer.

She forced her mind back on the task at hand and looked down into the pot.

"See, the lumps are disappearing already." She raised her eyes to his, a pleased smile on her lips. "We'll make a chef out of you yet," she promised. *Now* was the time for corrections, she decided. "And next time, make sure you pour the flour in *slowly*. It won't form lumps that way."

"Next time," he muttered, wondering to himself if there really had to be a next time. This winning Brittany back campaign seemed like a great deal more trouble than he'd first anticipated. Oh, he didn't mind the wining and the dining—if dining meant eating out—and he could even take in stride the dancing and writing love letters. But this cooking business— well, he wasn't all that sure he really wanted to go that route.

He knew without having to ask that his father had never had to cook anything for his mother to win her over, or to get her to marry him. But then, his mother was far more easy-going than Brittany. And although even now she was a very pretty woman and must have been even more so when she had first caught his father's eye, he knew for a fact that his mother had never been drop-dead gorgeous like Brittany.

Blake resigned himself. Winning a special woman required going the extra mile—or more—and this was definitely that extra mile.

Standing beside him, her hair inadvertently brushing against his bare arm—he'd rolled up his sleeves when they had started this—Katie looked into the pot. She nodded, pleased.

"Looks like it's really coming along," she told him, referring to the consistency that they had finally achieved.

Why her praise really pleased him he wouldn't have been able to explain to anyone, not even himself. But it did. "Thanks."

She indicated the package on the counter she'd just taken out for him. "Now chop up the mushrooms and stir those in, too."

"Do I add them in slowly, too?" he asked, putting down the spatula and ripping open the package.

She grinned. "Doesn't matter. All they do is just shrink as they cook—and also add taste," she said, anticipating his next question, which would undoubtedly be why he was adding mushrooms if it didn't matter how they went in.

"Oh. Okay." Presented with a chopping board and the eight-ounce box of whole mushrooms, Blake went to work. Chopping was clearly his favorite part of cooking, she observed.

He glanced in her direction. "You have this all in your head, don't you? Recipes," he clarified in case she didn't know what he was referring to.

"There's not all that much to remember," she told him with a careless shrug, throwing out the empty paper box and plastic wrap.

She was selling herself short, he thought. Looking back, he realized that it wasn't the first time she'd done so, either. She had a habit of doing that. Modesty, he supposed. Something that Brittany wouldn't have known anything about, he mused.

"Still," he acknowledged, "that's pretty impressive."

It was all in how you looked at things, Katie thought. "You retain sales figures. Same thing."

In more ways than one, he thought. Or didn't she realize that? "You do, too," he pointed out.

Something akin to a tiny starburst nestled

into her chest. Blake had actually noticed her proficiency with sales figures. *Score one for the underdog.* Katie silently congratulated herself on the tiny gain she'd just made. Smiling, she absently gathered up the mushrooms he had just chopped and deposited them into the pot, making sure to distribute them evenly.

"I thought I was supposed to do everything by myself." The initial object, when she'd told him about it earlier, was for him to make the meal from start to finish with only a little verbal guidance from her, but nothing more.

"I won't tell if you don't," Katie said. "Deal?" And then, as if to seal it, she winked.

He had no idea why—maybe it was the heat in the kitchen, or his preoccupation that it all turn out right—but there was something about that wink that seemed to burrow straight into his gut like a whirling dervish. His stomach tighten so hard in response that for a second, he wasn't sure he could catch his breath.

What the hell was going on here?

Had to be the heat, he decided with conviction. Couldn't have had anything to do with the woman he had known all of his life, he silently argued. That would be just plain ridiculous.

"Deal," he muttered. He grabbed a large spoon and dipped it into the Stroganoff. "Wait," he said as she turned away. "You might as well try it." Pulling the spoon out again, he held it out to her.

Because there was steam rising from it, she blew on the spoon's contents, and again he felt his stomach tightening, this time yet another notch.

What the hell had gotten into him? He was acting like a simpering teenager—something he wasn't even when he *had* been a teenager.

Get a grip, damn it, Blake ordered himself.

The second Katie tasted the fruits of Blake's labor, her eyes instantly began to water. But it wasn't her eyes that were the problem. It was her mouth, which felt as if it was on fire. So much so that it was a full minute before she could successfully use her tongue. Even so, she was somewhat surprised that it hadn't burned off.

"What else did you put in here?" she wanted to know, her voice exceedingly raspy.

"Why? What's wrong?" he wanted to know, instantly concerned. When she didn't answer him immediately, Blake reviewed the list of ingredients, ending with, "and pepper."

"What kind of pepper?" she asked, the fire in her throat finally subsiding after she'd downed half a glass of water.

He looked at her blankly. "Pepper pepper," he said. "I don't know. There're kinds?" When she nodded, he picked up the small container he'd used and held it up. "I put a tablespoon of this in."

She looked at the label. Now it made sense. "The recipe calls for a dash of pepper," she told him. "*Not* a tablespoon and it was supposed to be *white* pepper, not cayenne pepper."

"What the hell is a dash?" he demanded, irritated with his mistake.

"A lot less than a tablespoon," she told him.

He frowned. "White pepper?" he repeated.

"Yes."

This all sounded Greek to him. "There's a difference?"

Katie took another long drink of water. She was beginning to feel human again. "There's a difference."

His frown deepened as he looked at the pot of gently simmering Stroganoff. "So you're saying it's ruined?"

Not if she could help it, she thought. "No, it's not ruined," she answered.

"But you were just spitting fire," he said.

She opened up another can of consommé— she'd bought backup quantities of everything. "We'll just have to add more consommé and more flour to dilute it."

Hopefully, she added silently as she proceeded to do exactly that, moving a great deal faster and with more confidence than he had just displayed. Once she had stirred everything in and restored the balance, she told him, "Unless you've burned something down to a charcoal bit, you can usually salvage it in some manner." There, that was a good color, she congratulated herself. "You just have to be creative."

"*You're* the creative one," he told her, then confessed with a shrug, "It's not my thing."

"It'll come to you," she promised as she went on stirring the revitalized Stroganoff. "No one knows this stuff when they first start out. Remember, you were the one who came up with the marketing strategy to land the Fontaine account when it looked pretty hopeless," she reminded him, doing her best to restore Blake's confidence.

She hated to see him down, even if having him bounce back meant she was sending him directly into Brittany's finely manicured clutches.

"That was a Hail Mary play," he recalled honestly.

"So is salvaging Stroganoff—except that people's jobs aren't hanging in the balance like they were with the Fontaine account. Yours was the far more creative save," she pointed out.

When he grinned, she knew she'd done her job.

He watched her move around the kitchen

and he couldn't help noting the way she handled everything with such assurance. He was never going to be that confident and he knew it. Maybe this was all just a waste of their time.

When she turned around to face him again, he asked, "Do I really have to learn how to cook?"

She could hear the resistance in his voice. "Think of it as a last resort," she promised. And then she smiled. "You'll no doubt dazzle her with that footwork you've been working on. But if that fails, knowing how to whip up a good meal isn't really such a bad backup plan." She paused to take a taste of the now-salvaged Stroganoff. *Thank God.* "Here, you try," she coaxed, holding up the ladle that she'd filled for him.

Anticipating disaster, Blake took a very tiny, tentative taste, hardly touching his lips to the contents of the ladle. When they didn't fall off, he took another, decent-size sample this time. Surprise spread through him faster than the food.

"Hey," he cried, pleased, "not bad."

"No, not bad at all," she agreed, putting the ladle down on the spoon rest. "See? I told you. You really *can* cook."

There was a big leap between what he could do and what she had accomplished and he was smart enough to see the difference. "No, I can throw ingredients together. *You* can cook," he pointed out.

She wasn't about to stand here and argue with him, especially since, for the time being, he was right. "Let's just call it a joint project," she proposed. "And now, since this is ready," she indicated the pot, "why don't we have lunch?"

Eating something that he had actually prepared—or at least had had a hand in preparing—was rather a novel concept for him and the idea intrigued him. "Sure, why not? And after that, I'm going to be heading back to the hospital. I promised Wendy," he reminded Katie.

Since there was nothing pressing for her to attend to, she welcomed the idea of going back to see her friend. "Mind if I hitch a ride with you?"

His eyes met hers just before he helped himself to a generous portion of their joint effort. "Don't mind at all."

The way he said it warmed up her insides far more than the Stroganoff.

"Why can't we go in?"

John Michael Fortune's deep voice boomed up and down the corridor as he directed the annoyed question at the very young, very inexperienced-looking nurse standing beside his wife. Still a very handsome man at sixty-two, his six-foot-four, athletic frame made him seem even more imposing than he already was. The deep frown on his aristocratic face didn't help, either. Grown men were known to cower before the expression that was presently on his face. Virginia, his wife of thirty-six years, merely looked passed it and waited for the storm to blow over. It always did.

The young nurse took her cue from her.

"I did *not* drop everything and fly out all this way just to stand outside my daughter's hospital door," he declared, glaring at the closed door. "I came here to *see* her."

"And you will, Mr. Fortune," the nurse was quick to assure him. "Just as soon as the doctor is through examining her. It really shouldn't be much longer," she added nervously.

Accustomed to getting his way, John Michael was about to push his way past the little bit of a thing standing in front of him. Her words made him abruptly stop dead in his tracks.

"Examining her?" he echoed. "Well, why didn't you say so?" he demanded, more flustered than angry this time. "Damn it, girl, I almost walked in on my own daughter and embarrassed us both."

Relief flooded over the young woman's pale features. "But you didn't, and I did—say so, sir," she quickly tacked on when her patient's father looked at her quizzically.

Just then, the door behind her opened and with an even greater look of relief than a moment ago, the nurse stepped off to the side. She didn't have to be told that if she so much as hesitated even for a slight second, she ran the very real risk of getting trampled on by a man who allowed nothing to get in his way.

Nodding curtly at the physician who emerged, John Michael muttered, "It's about time," under his breath but loud enough for anyone within ten feet of him to hear. There was no doubt that the departing doctor heard.

The head of the Fortune clan, followed by the rest of the family that had flown out with him, strode into the room and crossed directly over to his daughter's hospital bed.

"You look pale," he observed.

"Must be the lighting in here," Wendy countered, then, because she had never been afraid to speak her mind, she admonished her father and said, "I heard you all the way in here, Dad. *With* the door closed."

If she was trying to make him express regret, she should have known better and just saved her breath.

"Good. I wanted you to know we were out there," he told his youngest child in his no-nonsense voice. And then he paused to look at her more closely. She really did look pale. "How are you feeling?"

Her mouth curved. "Much better, Dad," she replied. "Hi, Mom," she said as Virginia, the complete epitome of Southern gentility, leaned over and brushed a soft kiss against her cheek. Straightening, Virginia paused to push Wendy's hair away from her face in an old, familiar gesture that went all the way back to when she was a little girl whose bangs were always falling into her eyes.

John Michael, oblivious to the fact that his other children all had questions for Wendy, nodded as he leaned in closer. His very manner reduced the room down to only the two of them.

"No aftereffects? Everything okay?" he pressed in a slightly gentler tone that still, for all intents and purposes, sounded businesslike.

"Yes, Dad, everything's okay. Honest," she underscored when he raised his eyebrows as if he intended to grill her, the way he had when he'd caught her sneaking into the house after two in the morning. She'd just turned eighteen at the time.

"And the baby?" he wanted to know.

"Yes, how is she?" Virginia asked, adding her soft voice to the chorus.

"She's fine, too. Just a little small, so they're going to keep Mary Anne here in the hospital for a little while, make sure everything's going well." She said it so matter-of-factly, no one would guess that the thought of leaving her little girl behind when she went home tomorrow was all but killing her.

"So you really did have a girl, huh," John Michael said. He gave the impression that he'd thought perhaps the amniocentesis had been wrong.

Wendy did her best to hide her amusement. "Yes, Dad, she's a girl."

"And her name is Mary Anne."

She could hear her father's disappointment. "Don't worry, Dad. She's not going to be an only child. If the next one's a boy, maybe we'll name it after you."

Her father nodded, brightening at the possibility and trying not to show it. "You could do worse."

Virginia Fortune smiled at her daughter. "I think Mary Anne's a lovely name. I know I like it."

"Her name could be 'mud,' for all it matters," her sister Emily said with feeling.

The rest of the family all turned to look at her. Ever since the tornado had wreaked such havoc for all of them, Emily had been acting a little off center, but no one wanted to mention it, hoping that it would pass. They were all coping with the event in their own way and were cutting one another slack.

Still, this was something that Virginia felt needed to be commented on. "Emily, that's just an awful name," her mother cried, appalled.

"What matters," Emily continued as if nothing was said, "is that she's healthy."

"I agree with Em," Michael chimed in.

John Michael shrugged his broad, thin shoulders. "Well, apparently we don't have a say in the name," he commented, still reflecting on the fact that his first grandchild would not bear any part of the family name.

Wendy braced herself to offer a defense of her choice, "Dad—"

But her father held his hands up to stop her protest before it was launched. "Hey, I said it wasn't a bad name," he reminded her.

Just then, the door to her room opened again and she immediately looked in that direction, hoping for reinforcements or a diversion. Her father had a way of belaboring a point if it suited him.

When she saw Blake and Katie walking in, the relief she felt was overwhelming. "You came back."

Blake crossed to her bed and positioned himself beside her—and across from his father. "Said we would," he told her.

Katie noted that he'd said "we," when this morning, he had promised that only he would return. Was this progress? Or just the effects of too much cayenne pepper? she wondered wryly.

Either way, she savored it for a moment, telling herself that at least she had that.

Chapter 12

Within a few minutes, as they surrounded her bed, the sound of Wendy's family's voices began to grow and swell, until they were all but deafening. They were each vying for her attention.

Virginia attempted, rather unsuccessfully, to keep the volume down. After a few more minutes had passed and the decibel level continued to climb, it was inevitable that the noise would attract someone's attention. And it did.

Ten minutes into their visit, a tall, heavyset and seasoned nurse with the bearing of a drill sergeant stuck her head into the overcrowded single care unit and did a quick assessment of the situation.

Walking in, she announced, "There're way too many people in this room. I'm afraid you're going to have to take turns visiting with the new mama." Her tone left no leeway for argument.

Nonetheless, Wendy's father drew himself up to his full and rather intimidating height, then scowled down at her. She looked to be approximately ten inches shorter. "Young woman, do you know who I am?"

Meeting his steely gaze, she looked completely unfazed. "One of the people who's going to be waiting outside for his turn at the new mother's bedside," the nurse replied matter-of-factly.

The steely glare narrowed into slits. "I'm John Michael Fortune," he informed her coldly, "and I recently made a sizable donation to this hospital because they took such good care of my daughter when she went into premature labor."

"Did you, now?" For a split second, it looked as if the nurse was going to relent and back away, but then she merely nodded. "All right, then you get to be one of the ones who gets first crack at visiting, but I still need half of you to wait outside."

Ever the peacemaker, Katie quickly moved to the front of the group and said to them,

"Why don't I show all of you the way to the nursery so you can meet the cutest baby you'll ever hope to see," she suggested, looking from one of Wendy's siblings to another.

Emily spoke up first, crossing to Katie. She hooked her arms through Katie's, as if to seal the deal. "I'd love to see the baby."

She said it with such feeling that, along with her earlier comment, Blake caught himself wondering if something was going on with his sister. He started to leave with the others.

But Wendy wanted him to run interference for her with their father. Ordinarily, she was more than up to it, but the delivery had literally and figuratively taken a great deal out of her and she needed an ally on her side—just in case.

"You just got here," Wendy protested, her eyes pinning Blake in place for a second.

He smiled at her. "I'll be back soon," he promised. "Besides, I don't want to monopolize you. The others haven't had a chance to talk to you yet—and we wouldn't want to upset your nurse now, would we?" he asked, smiling just a little too brightly at the woman waiting by the doorway. Their eyes met as he passed her on his way out.

The woman's expression never changed.

"Not if you know what's good for you," she replied in a low, even voice.

Blake wisely kept to himself the laugh that bubbled up in response.

He caught up to Emily a couple of steps outside the room and fell into step beside her as Katie led the small cluster of Atlanta Fortunes down the hallway to the nursery. It occurred to Blake, out of the blue, that he would probably be lost without Katie. She seemed to anticipate whatever needed doing before anything was said and had a knack of heading off problems before they actually became problems. The woman was worth her weight in gold.

And right now, she'd cleared the playing field for him so that he could talk to Emily alone.

"Something wrong?" he asked Emily in a hushed, lowered voice.

He noticed that she stiffened ever so slightly. "Why do you ask?"

He didn't beat around the bush. "Because you don't sound quite like the cheerful Emily I know. You're okay, right?" He peered at her face and saw nothing to enlighten him. "No ill aftereffects from that little dustup with the tornado the other month?" he pressed.

"Is this you, being the concerned brother?" Emily asked, amused.

"Something like that," he conceded, then asked, "What's up?"

She sighed as they turned a corner. How did she phrase this without sounding strange? For a second, she pressed her lips together, debating just shrugging it off. But this was Blake and although they'd had their share of teasing—not to mention fights—they were close and she had never lied to him, at least not deliberately. Now didn't seem like a good time to start.

She began slowly, like a child dipping a toe into the icy ocean tide. "The tornado got me thinking."

"A lot of that going around," Blake assured his sister. After all, if it hadn't been for the tornado, he wouldn't have realized that he had let the opportunity of his lifetime slip through his fingers without doing anything about it. "So, this thinking you did, where did it lead you?" he asked.

God, she never thought she would be saying this. Or *feeling* this. And yet, here she was, filled with this insatiable longing that was ripping her apart.

Emily took a breath and dove in. "I realized I wanted a baby." She looked at him. He didn't look surprised—or even amused. She decided that he couldn't really be getting the full import of what she was telling him. Suddenly, it became important to her that he understand. "Badly. I want a baby badly—like that's all I've been able to think of."

Emily was older than he was. As far as he knew, there was no steady man in her life and maybe she was hearing her biological clock ticking—maybe the tornado had even set it off. He could sympathize with that.

"Stop thinking and do something about it," he counseled.

She blinked. She hadn't known what to expect from him as a reaction, but this certainly threw her.

"What?"

"*Do* something about it," he repeated. "Get a plan. Something with teeth, like a campaign strategy." He thought for a moment, then threw out various choices for her. "You could adopt, hire a surrogate, or go aggressively after the man of your dreams with the goal of starting a family. Those are just three options. But whatever route you decide is best for you, *go and do it*. Sitting and sighing and wishing isn't going to get you anywhere. It certainly isn't going to help you get a baby."

Stunned, Emily looked at him. And then she smiled. "You know, for a younger brother, you didn't turn out half bad."

Blake held his hands up, as if to fend off her words. "Please, you'll make my head swell."

When she laughed, she sounded like her old self again. He knew then that she was going to be all right. And that he had succeeded in getting through to his sister. He had a very strong feeling that she was going to take his advice.

He watched her at the nursery window as she looked, not just at her new niece, but at all the other babies as well. There was love in Emily's eyes. Love and wistfulness. Emily wasn't just talking, she really wanted a baby.

Wow.

Quite unintentionally, his eyes met Katie's as she glanced toward him over her shoulder. There was the woman who was going to help him attain his own goal, Blake thought with growing affection. It was getting to the point that he honestly didn't know what he would ever do without her.

At times the thought struck him that he didn't know how he could have gotten so lucky. It was as if Katie could almost read his mind, knowing what he needed before he even did. There weren't many working relationships like that—or even regular relationships for that matter, he thought. She was, quite possibly, the total package. Smart, competent and beautiful to boot.

Was it his imagination, or had she gotten, well, *more* beautiful of late? Or was that just a result of their spending so much more time together? He wasn't sure. All he knew was that the past few days he'd become more…aware of her than usual. He caught himself looking at her as if he'd never seen her before.

Had to be the close proximity, he decided. They'd all but been in each other's pockets of late.

The next moment, his thoughts took off in another direction. He had to find a way to thank her for all the extra time she'd put in on this unorthodox project of his. It was only right. After all, there was nothing in her contract that said she had to help him find a way to capture his future wife's heart. That was going above and beyond.

One in a million, that was Katie Wallace, he thought. Smiling at her, he nodded absently.

It was hard for her not to lose her train of thought when he looked at her like that. But she couldn't just begin babbling, at least not when his older brothers and sisters were around her like this. They'd think she was crazy—which she was, she silently acknowledged. Crazy in love with Blake.

And once he's with Brittany, you'll just be certifiably crazy, nothing more, she told herself with sick resignation. *Face it, that day is coming, and soon. You can't keep burying your head in the sand like this forever.*

She pushed the thought aside. Later—she'd deal with the inevitable later. Right now, she had Blake's siblings to contend with.

"I can't tell you how good it is to be back in my own bed again," Wendy said with yet another deep, contented sigh. It was two days later and Marcos and Katie had brought her home after she'd been discharged. There was only one thing to mar her happiness. "Everything would be perfect if I could have brought the baby home with me, too."

"She'll be here soon enough," Katie told her reassuringly. She sat on the edge of Wendy's huge bed, the way she used to when they were younger and sharing secrets they were sure no one else knew. "If I were you, I'd get all the rest and sleep I could now, because there won't be any once Mary Anne is here—since you turned down your father's offer to hire a nurse to help you," she reminded her friend.

Wendy shook her head. "I want to be a hands-on mother," she said with determination, "not an occasional one."

"Still, it wouldn't be a bad idea to have someone here just part-time," Katie advised. "Just until you get the hang of the routine. No one would think any less of you," she promised, knowing how Wendy's mind worked. "This is your first time as the mother of a newborn and every little thing's going to seem like a crisis to you until you get used to the routine—and, more importantly, to the aberrations."

"How do you know so much?" Wendy asked with a mystified laugh.

Katie shrugged. She supposed that she did come off a little like a know-it-all. "I just read a lot, that's all."

Wendy inclined her head, leaning closer to Katie. "Okay, I'll keep my options open. To be honest, Marcos said something along the same lines," she admitted. "But I want to try to do this on my own first."

Katie gave her friend an alternate choice. "You know, I could hang around, pitch in for a while if you like. I don't have anything pressing to do anymore."

"What about Project Brittany?" Wendy asked. "Has Blake finally come to his senses and decided to scrap that?"

Katie did her best to look as if the thought of Blake cozying up to Brittany didn't tear her apart the way that it did.

"Well, the fund-raiser that he wants to take Brittany to is this coming weekend and he feels that he's fairly well prepared to get his campaign underway." Each word she uttered felt like a sharp pin pricking her heart. "So there's no more plotting a course of action for him," she told Wendy. And then she sighed. "As a matter of fact, he wants to show me his gratitude by taking me out to dinner tomorrow night."

"Tomorrow night?" Wendy repeated, her eyes widening as she said the words slowly.

"Yes, tomorrow night." Katie stared at her friend's expression. "Why do you look like that?"

It was Wendy's turn to stare—in disbelief. "Katie, don't you know what tomorrow is?"

Since she had gotten here, it felt as if the days just fed into one another, especially after all the drama that had occurred with the way Wendy's baby had been born. She thought for a minute, then said hesitantly, "Thursday?"

"It's Valentine's Day. Blake wants to take you out on *Valentine's Day*," Wendy emphasized.

Wendy was right, Katie realized. Tomorrow *was* Valentine's Day. But she had her doubts that Blake had been aware of that when he'd made the offer. "I'm sure that he doesn't realize that."

Wendy drew herself up as best she could, given that she was still in bed. "We'll *make* him realize it."

"We?" And just how was Wendy going to hope to accomplish that when Katie was the one who would be going out with Blake?

Wendy's smile was wide and dazzling in its confidence. "We," she affirmed. "Go to my closet," she instructed. It was impossible to miss her enthusiasm. "I have just the dress for you to wear."

Fifteen minutes later, Wendy was shifting impatiently in her bed. "Well, come out," she coaxed, raising her voice to carry through the bathroom door. "I want to see what it looks like on you."

In her opinion, Katie was taking an inordinate amount of time putting on the sexy black dress that she had selected for her.

Reluctantly, Katie finally opened the door and came out, moving very hesitantly.

"Where's the rest of it?" Katie wanted to know.

The slinky, black dress was clinging to her every curve. It only came down to her thighs and, although it had long, narrow sleeves that ended at her wrists and hinted at modesty, all hints vanished when she turned around. The dress was completely backless.

"There's just enough to make it interesting," Wendy told her. "Damn, but you look gorgeous!" she cried with no little pride. "And

I've got just the shoes to go with that. A great pair of strappy high heels," she elaborated, then cocked her head as she studied Katie's reflection in the wardrobe mirror Katie was facing. "I'm going to have to fix your hair for you," Wendy said. It wasn't an offer, it was a given. One that made her grin in anticipation. "One look at you and that brother of mine is going to say, 'Brittany who?'"

Not from the way he talked about her, Katie thought. Although she hated raining on Wendy's parade, she didn't want to give her best friend false hope, either. "I really, really doubt that."

"I don't," Wendy countered cheerfully and with the confidence of a person who was seldom wrong. "Now, remember, when you enter the restaurant, walk as if every man in the room is looking at you."

"If I think that, I'm not going to be able to take a single step," she protested.

"Yes, you are," Wendy told her firmly, "because you know that every one of those men looking at you is living in the moment—and envying my big brother like hell." There was pure joy in Wendy's eyes. "This is going to be magnificent!" she prophesied gleefully, clasping her hands together in anticipation.

Katie tried her best to smile and ignore the

full squadron of butterflies that had suddenly shown up as she began to earnestly think about tomorrow evening and all the different possible ways that she could embarrass herself.

Blake had chosen Red for his dinner with Katie, because he was familiar with it and because Marcos was the manager, so he knew the food was always excellent.

What he obviously *wasn't* familiar with, he thought ruefully, was the ordinary calendar. He'd been so busy with the campaign and with learning all the different things that Katie had come up with to help him win Brittany's heart, he'd somehow remained totally oblivious to the fact that today was Valentine's Day.

How could he have been this blind? He hadn't even sent Brittany a card. If his plan had only gone a little faster, he would have taken her out on the big day instead of having dinner with Katie. Well, there was nothing he could do about it now, he thought with resignation.

He was definitely going to have to pick up something to give to Brittany as a gift at the fund-raiser. A belated Valentine's Day present, he thought wryly. He knew without being told that women didn't like being forgotten on this all-important day. But there was still Saturday. He managed to convince himself that it would be more surprising that way. Brittany definitely wouldn't be expecting a Valentine's Day gift three days after the actual day had gone by.

Maybe a pair of diamond earrings would do the trick.

No, diamond earrings would be too common a present for someone like Brittany. No doubt she probably owned at least half a dozen pairs.

He'd ask Katie, he decided.

Katie had had her fingers on the pulse of this thing right from the beginning—she'd know what kind of a gift to suggest to him. No point in his racking his brain about it now.

Katie, he couldn't help thinking with more than a trace of admiration, seemed to be up on just about everything. Lucky thing she had decided to come work for him when she graduated rather than pick some other, possibly more lucrative firm. Otherwise, who knew if he could even begin to pull this off? Her suggestions had been invaluable.

Because of her, he was more than confident that he was going to be successful. This time next week, Brittany and he would be back together and very possibly on their way to planning a wedding.

Blake glanced at his watch. Katie should have been here by now.

Where was she?

It wasn't like her to be late. She was usually early. He had offered to pick her up, as usual, but Wendy had insisted that he go on to the restaurant, pick out a table and wait for Katie there. She'd told him that Marcos would bring Katie with him when he returned from his break. Since she'd come home from the hospital, he looked at every break as an opportunity to drive home and look in on her.

Had to be nice, Blake mused, to be in love that way. He wanted what Wendy and Marcos had. What Scott and Christina had.

He wanted a woman to love who loved him back.

He wanted Brittany.

Growing a tad impatient, Blake scanned the dining area, looking to see if Katie had arrived yet. But the only woman he saw walking in was a really hot-looking young woman who appeared, at least from where he was sitting, as if she was loaded for bear. She was certainly turning heads as she moved through the room.

Some guy was really going to have his socks knocked off tonight, Blake mused as he continued scanning the immediate area.

Okay, so *where* was Katie?

Most of the tables were full. The entire dining area was filled with couples.

And him, alone, he thought, darkly.

Maybe he should just postpone this, take Katie out to dinner some other time when there was more light available, he thought philosophically.

Tonight the tastefully decorated restaurant seemed fairly dim, due to the fact that a tall, white candle burned brightly in the center of each table. Including his.

Blake rose to his feet. He was going to go find Marcos and leave a message with him for Katie. Maybe Katie hadn't even come with Marcos, but if that was the case, wouldn't Marcos have come to tell him that? Of course, maybe they were stuck in traffic.

Preoccupied, Blake pushed in his chair.

Maybe—

"Hi, Blake, you're not leaving, are you? Am I that late?"

Recognizing her voice, Blake turned to answer Katie and the words dried up on his tongue, along with his ability to draw a sufficient breath. The sexy woman he'd noticed walking into the dining area just a couple of seconds ago had just walked up to his table— and him.

She was Katie.

Chapter 13

"Katie?" Blake heard himself asking uncertainly. "Is that you?"

"Of course it's me," she said, sliding easily into the chair opposite his. "I am the only one you asked to meet you here tonight, right?" And then she looked up at him and saw the strange expression on his face. As if he was still trying to place her. "Why are you looking at me like that? Do I have a smudge on my face or a leaf in my hair?" she asked.

As she spoke, she shrugged off the shawl she had wrapped around her shoulders. The weather outside, blessedly, was unseasonably warm right now, but she was still a bit chilly in this dress that Wendy had insisted in no uncertain terms that she wear. Marcos had let her off right at the door, but that was still enough time for the evening breeze to find her and weave itself around her naked back.

She had to admit that the look in Blake's eyes did go a long way in heating her up again.

Katie leaned forward over the table. "Blake?" she prodded when he remained silent.

An uneasiness began to spread through her. Oh, who was she kidding? She was playing dress-up in fancy clothes that no more fit her personality than a leopard-skin bikini. He probably looked that way because he was trying not to laugh. She felt a blush creeping up her neck.

"*Say* something," she begged, unable to endure the silence much longer.

Blake leaned back in his chair as if he had been punched in the gut and was only now able to react. "Wow."

That wasn't the something she was expecting to hear. "Excuse me?"

"Wow," Blake repeated, unable to tear his eyes away from her. Half words were flashing in and out of his head like Fourth of July fireworks. "You look—wow," was all he could manage.

The silver tongue he had developed over the years was nothing more than a lead weight in his mouth right now as words continued to completely elude him. All he could think was that she was absolutely gorgeous.

How could he have missed that?

He'd seen her practically every day for the past two years, had known her since she was a gangly kid, playing dress-up with Wendy and staging sleepovers. When had all this happened?

He felt like Rip van Winkle, waking up to a whole brand-new world.

"Thank you," Katie murmured uncertainly. Still feeling self-conscious and not knowing what to do with her hands, when she saw a goblet of wine next to her plate, she gratefully reached for it.

Blake momentarily came to. "Oh, I told the waiter it was all right to pour the wine," he said, and then gave a small, self-deprecating laugh. "I don't even know if you drink wine," he admitted. By the time he finished his sentence, she had already raised the goblet to her lips and drank deeply, emptying half the contents. "I guess you do." He smiled to himself and then raised his goblet. "To surprises," he said just before he sampled his own wine.

Feeling oddly loose and at ease now, Katie asked, "Did you order dinner, too?"

"No," he answered quickly, then explained,

"I didn't order anything else because I wasn't sure what you'd like to eat."

He usually had far less trouble talking, he upbraided himself. Even with strangers. Why was he tripping on his tongue now, with Katie of all people? She was just like another sister to him. He realized that he was watching the way her chest moved as she breathed—well, maybe not *quite* like a sister, he amended.

"Marcos tells me that everything on the menu is excellent," he added awkwardly.

"So I hear," she replied just before she took another long sip of wine from her glass.

She found, to her delight, that her nerves were no longer jumping around quite so much and that an easy, happy calm had begun to descend over her. This was much better, she thought.

Opening the menu, she scanned the two sides, then turned a page. While she was deciding, the waiter, on his way to another table with a full bottle of wine, paused over her goblet, a silent query in his manner.

Ordinarily, she didn't drink at all, but what the heck? she thought, stifling an unexpected giggle that rose to her lips. This was Valentine's Day, wasn't it? And most likely, her first and last dinner with Blake before he became part of the duo of Blake and Brittany, or, more likely, Brittany and Blake. Either way, he was going to be forbidden fruit to her.

"Yes, please," she said in response to the waiter's silent question, moving her goblet closer to him. The waiter filled her goblet, then automatically did the same with Blake's.

It was then that Blake realized he must have emptied his own goblet without even being aware of it. He was apparently *that* mesmerized by this new version of Katie—or had she just been downplaying what she looked like all these years?

He really didn't know.

He was staring and that was rude, he scolded himself.

Forcing himself to relax, he said, "You know, I really want to thank you for putting up with all this." Katie raised her eyes to his, a surprised expression on her face. That made two of them, he thought. He hadn't realized he was going to phrase his thanks just that way until the words were out of his mouth. He needed to rephrase that.

"I mean…" His voice trailed off as he searched for the right words.

The search came up empty. His mind was just not functioning tonight, he realized in no small frustration. It wasn't functioning, he knew, because completely alien thoughts kept insisting on getting in the way. Alien thoughts such as wondering if that one time he'd kissed Katie and she had brought his world to its knees had been a fluke.

There was, of course, only one way to find out, but he wasn't all that sure she would welcome being kissed by him again. After all, she had just spent all this time helping him with his campaign to land the woman of his dreams. Having him kiss her might make her angry....

He blinked, looking hard at Katie. *Was* Brittany really the woman of his dreams, or was he just caught up in this whole thing because he felt she was an opportunity he'd lost? Was it the whole "you want what you can't have" syndrome, or—?

Or what? he demanded the next moment, his thoughts growing progressively fuzzier and utterly unfocused. What *was* focused was all centered around Katie.

Why hadn't he noticed that her eyes were like warm chocolate before? He had a weakness for warm chocolate. And cream. Her skin reminded him of cream.

Did it taste like cream?

What the hell was going on with him?

Why was he looking at her like that? Katie wondered. As though he wanted to be with her, when this dinner was supposedly to thank her for the big help she'd been to him these past few weeks? Right, she was helping the man she loved win the heart of another woman— a woman who was never going to care about Blake the way that she could. The way she *did*.

Katie opened her mouth to say just that, but then stopped.

What did it matter?

Blake loved Brittany. He *wanted* Brittany and he was going to go *after* Brittany no matter what she said or did. Hell, she could stand on top of this table and proclaim her feelings for Blake at the top of her lungs and it would make no difference—except maybe to get him to run out of the restaurant as fast as he could.

She might as well just enjoy this meal— when had she ordered it? she wondered, looking at her plate. And when had she almost finished it?

She couldn't remember.

Couldn't remember finishing her glass of wine, either, she realized. Was it just one, or had she had a second? She tried to think and remember—and then decided that it wasn't worth the effort. And it didn't matter, she told herself again. She wasn't driving.

Smiling to herself, content with the moment, Katie played with the stem of her goblet, moving it back and forth between her fingertips.

She was simply enjoying the warm, rosy feeling that was spreading through her.

With effort, she tried to concentrate on what Blake was saying. It wouldn't do to have him think that she was ignoring him.

"Excuse me?" she said, hoping he'd repeat what he'd just said, because somehow his words had all vanished without registering.

How was that possible?

"I said I'm worried about Jordana," he repeated. He'd had occasion to talk to Jordana at the hospital when she came to see the baby and he came away with the feeling that something was definitely wrong with his older sister. "I tried talking to her at the hospital, but she seemed preoccupied—and a little off," he admitted. There didn't seem to be a better way to phrase that.

Katie nodded, then thought that maybe he wanted her to say something in response. She grasped at the first thing she could remember and hoped it made sense. Hoped that *she* made sense. Because right now, her brain felt like a bowl of cold spaghetti.

"Maybe it's because of the tornado." She paused, then thought that maybe that didn't make sense all by itself, so she continued. "Maybe coming so close to death made her take another look at her life."

There, that sounded better, Katie congratulated herself.

Blake rolled her words over in his head, then nodded. "Maybe."

Her mouth curved. Yea! She'd said the right thing. And then another thought danced through her head. Maybe if she said, "Kiss me," he would. The thought had just popped into her head out of nowhere, but when it did, she liked it. Liked it a lot.

She drew her shoulders back, about to make the suggestion when he cut her off.

"Well, I'd better take you home," he said out of the blue.

Surprised, she felt disoriented for a second. They had been eating just a minute ago. Why did he want to leave? Was it something she'd said? She tried to think—and couldn't.

"Oh. Okay," she murmured, trying to pull her shawl from the back of the chair. She was unsuccessful. It was stuck.

Rising to his feet, Blake moved behind her to help her with her shawl. It was then that he got a really good look at her back—as well as the lack of material at that portion of the dress. He felt his stomach do a few involuntary flips, then tighten really, really hard.

The effects of the wine he'd had at dinner had long since dissipated, but this made him think that perhaps they weren't completely gone after all. Either that or he was getting intoxicated in a whole new way that he never had before.

With the bill taken care of, despite his brother-in-law's protests—how could this be a "thank you for all you've done" dinner for Katie if Marcos was the one who paid for it?—Blake took her arm and gently guided Katie through the maze of tables and to the front door.

Pushing the heavy mahogany door open, they walked out and were immediately met by an evening breeze that was far chillier than it had been earlier.

As if instinctively, Katie huddled against him, which in turn caused all sorts of havoc in the pit of his stomach again—as well as parts beyond.

That was when he realized that the effects from the wine really had completely dissipated, but the effects from Katie were definitely intensifying. There was no getting away from it. She was a beautiful woman and he was attracted to her.

But he couldn't act on that attraction, or even explore it. It wouldn't be fair to her, or Brittany. Right?

It was an argument that had no winning side, he realized.

Instead, Blake focused on getting Katie back to Wendy's house and himself back to Scott's. The first part of that was easy enough.

But then, that was where things began to suddenly stall.

At the front door, Katie turned and looked up at him with wide, innocent eyes just before she turned the key in the lock.

"Why don't you come in for a little while?" she suggested.

He was debating the pros and cons of that when he suddenly found himself being playfully pulled across the threshold and into the semidark house.

Marcos, he knew, was still at the restaurant. That meant that his sister was home by herself.

"Maybe I can look in on Wendy," he agreed, even as he was doing his best not to think how damn sexy Katie looked in that black dress.

The winter-white shawl had managed to dip down, exposing her nude back. More than anything, he wanted to run his hand along her skin....

And that perfume she was wearing—had she worn it all along, or was this something new? Whatever it was, it was causing him to be exceedingly aware of every move she made.

It occurred to him that he had been relatively oblivious to the woman who, for the past two hours, had been occupying center stage in his thoughts. In his world.

He walked up the stairs like a man caught up in a dream.

He promised himself that once he started talking to Wendy, whatever it was that was wrong with him would pass. But when he came up to Wendy's door, he found that it was closed. That meant that his sister was either asleep, or almost asleep. Either way, he was not about to disturb her.

What he needed to do, he silently told himself, was to get a grip and to man up.

Turning away from his sister's door, he wound up brushing up against Katie, who was standing directly behind him—much too close for his comfort. It was time to take a stand.

What Blake fully intended to do when he took hold of Katie's shoulders was to gently move her back and then aside so that he could go back downstairs and leave. He'd had absolutely no intention of drawing Katie to him so that she was even closer than before.

And he certainly hadn't thought he was going to lower his head so that his lips could touch hers.

And absolutely under *no* circumstances did he have any intention of kissing her.

But she was and they did and he was.

Moreover, he couldn't stop, even when deep down inside of him, he knew that stopping was the right thing to do.

Without knowing quite how, he swept Katie away from Wendy's bedroom door and somehow wound up moving down the hallway to the guest bedroom that she was currently occupying.

His lips never left hers during that whole time.

And all he was really aware of was that the more he kissed Katie, the more he not just *wanted* to kiss her but *needed* to kiss her. And the more he desperately desired her.

If this continued—

No, it *couldn't* continue.

With effort, Blake pulled his head back, breaking the connection between them. He saw the bewildered look in her eyes and felt that it clearly mirrored what he was feeling inside at the moment. Not that he could afford to share that with her.

"Katie," he whispered, "we have to stop—"

She wanted to shout: *No, we don't*, but she settled on a single word: "Why?"

The simple question completely threw him for a second.

Why?

Well, God knew *he* certainly didn't want to

stop. It was for her sake, not his own, that he had pulled away. Couldn't she see that?

"Because if we don't," he told her truthfully, choosing his words slowly, "I'm going to wind up making love to you."

She searched his face, still unable to see why he would stop cold like that, just when her body temperature had reached the boiling point.

"And you don't want to?" she guessed, her eyes intently on his.

"Don't want to?" he echoed incredulously. How could she possibly think that? He was struggling to make the supreme sacrifice and she thought he was just passing the time of day here? Was she just pretending to return his kisses with fervor? Didn't she know what was going on inside of him? "It's the only thing I *do* want right now." he swore.

Katie smiled at that. Smiled in such a way that he could literally *feel* her smile right down to his very toes. Moreover, it jarred him as if he'd just stood in the path of a kicking mule.

The next moment, he heard her murmur, "Well, then?" just before she sealed her lips to his. Just before she sealed his fate.

The matter was no longer in his hands. He was on board a runaway train, clinging to the side of it for all he was worth, as heat, passion and desire roared through his veins, clamoring for tribute.

For fulfillment.

Even as every fiber of his being seemed to all but shout out for her.

The door to Katie's bedroom stood open, a silent invitation to them.

It didn't go unheeded.

They all but tumbled across the threshold and into her room. Blake was only vaguely aware of closing the door with his elbow. It was the only part of his body that wasn't consumed with showing Katie just how very much he desired her. Even as she filled every inch of his senses, of his soul, he craved even more.

The slinky, come-hither dress she had on fell to the floor after only a couple of tugs, leaving her clad in a black lacy thong and her strappy high heels, bathed in the heat of his desire.

One pull and the thong was no more. With her arms wrapped around his neck, Katie stepped out of the shoes. Only his desire remained steadfast, clinging to her skin like the hazy moisture from a sauna.

Yes, oh yes, her mind cried over and over again as she eagerly pulled at his clothing, tugging first his open jacket, then his shirt off his shoulders until they were both on the floor in a heap.

She fumbled with the belt at his trim, hard waist, then with surer fingers coaxed away the fabric from his thighs until those garments, too, joined the rest of his clothing on the floor.

His desire for her was clearly evident and every fiber in her being silently cheered as her anticipation mounted.

His lips were hot on her skin, kissing her everywhere, making the fog in her spinning brain widen until it completely swallowed her up as she felt the thrust of his tongue along the most sensitive part of her.

For her, there was nothing and no one, only Blake. Only this feeling that he had created within her, this feeling that was now exploding inside of her over and over again.

She frantically wanted to race to a climax, but at the same time, she wanted to hold it back, hold it back and savor this because even in her revelry, even with the wine coloring everything, there was a small part of her that thought, that *knew*, that something this wondrous might never happen again.

With all her heart, she wanted to freeze time, or, at the very least, make it progress in slow motion. So she reined herself in, lavishing kisses along his neck and chest the same way he had done to her. Reveling in the fact that his breathing had grown as labored as hers.

The sound filled her head even as demands and desires pounded all through her.

And then he was over her, pressing her into the bed, his weight hovering over her like the promise of rainbows in the rain. Her breath caught in her throat as he entered her, the movement as gentle as his first kiss had begun. And then, as with the kiss, the intensity grew, taking on width and breadth as the rhythm between them increased, growing in scope until that was all there was.

And then there was more.

Chapter 14

Her body still throbbing, Katie seriously began to doubt that she would ever be able to breathe normally again. But eventually, she finally managed to drag just enough air into her lungs to dispel the need to gasp and pant. Her chest ceased heaving.

As did his.

Her head was resting against his chest now and she felt the beat of Blake's heart beneath her cheek. The steady rhythm was infinitely comforting and she felt that if she could remain like this forever, she'd never want for anything else.

She had discovered bliss and this was it.

But it was inevitable that this was finite.

Blake shifted and she had to move, even if it was ever so slightly. The end of the interlude was drawing close. But just as a sadness began to unfurl within her, Katie felt his arm close around her and, just as when they'd first walked out of the restaurant an eternity ago, she curled into his arm, huddling into his warmth. Drawing her contentment from that.

She felt Blake draw in a deep breath and then he said her name as if it was a precursor to something she wasn't going to like.

"Katie—"

Warranted or not, survival instincts immediately kicked in. A very real fear took hold that he was going to say something that would negate what had just happened, or, at the very least, leech some of the starlight away from it. She didn't want to risk losing that, not just yet.

So when he said her name, Katie raised her head and placed her fingertips against his lips, momentarily silencing him.

"Shh," she begged. "Don't say anything. Not a word," she instructed softly just before she laid her head back down on his chest.

Closing her eyes, Katie allowed her mind to peacefully drift off and soon, the rest of her did, too. Before she realized it, she was asleep.

She slept, while Blake, enveloped in the darkness—they had never turned on light in the bedroom—dwelled on what had just transpired.

Dwelled on what he had done.

What had possessed him? he silently demanded. Where was his control? His common sense? Why hadn't he just walked her to the door and left her there? Why had he felt so compelled to test the waters of this brand-new environment he'd suddenly found himself in?

He looked down at the sleeping woman curled up against him and felt—heaven help him—fresh stirrings.

For Katie.

Suddenly, the simple had become so very complicated. And it was all his own fault.

The darker it grew outside the bedroom window, the darker his thoughts became.

Moving her shoulders, Katie stretched her body like a contented feline waking from a long, decadent nap. She realized that there was a smile on her face, a wide, guileless, happy smile even before she opened her eyes. Her smile had nothing to do with any dream and everything to do with what had happened before she had surrendered to sleep.

She stretched again and this time realized

that even though she was really extending her body to its limits, she wasn't coming in contact with anything other than sheets and part of a comforter.

She reached for Blake as she opened her eyes and discovered that she was reaching for someone who wasn't there.

"Blake?" she murmured.

When there was no reply, she said his name louder and turned her head in the direction of the bathroom. But there was no sound of running water, no sound of movement of any kind. The door to the bathroom stood wide open and she could see from where she was that there was no one inside the small room.

An uneasiness whispered along the perimeter of her throbbing head.

The wine, she remembered. She'd had too much wine.

Sitting up, Katie quickly scanned the bedroom. He wasn't there. And neither, she realized when she glanced down at the floor right before the bed, were Blake's clothes.

Had he quietly slipped out of bed, not wanting to wake her, gotten dressed and gone down for breakfast?

Katie realized that as she formed the question, it was accompanied by a prayer. Because if Blake hadn't gone down for breakfast, and he wasn't here, that meant that he'd left.

Left.

Left without even saying goodbye.

She didn't like the sound of that. A chill came over her heart as she suddenly remembered that he had a ticket for a flight out of San Antonio. A flight to Atlanta. She knew this because, as his assistant, she was the one who had made the reservation for him.

Katie moved as quickly as a woman whose head bordered on exploding could and threw on the first clothes she got her hands on. For the moment forgetting about such niceties as brushing her teeth or combing her hair, and ignoring the fact that she was barefoot, she ran out into the hall and all but crashed into the housekeeper.

Juanita Ruiz, a heavyset, motherly looking woman, was carrying a breakfast tray before her and stopped short just before Wendy's door. Quick thinking had her moving the tray out of range and saving her employer's breakfast.

"Are you all right, Katie?" the woman asked, concerned.

Katie didn't bother answering the question. She needed one of her own answered.

"Is Wendy's brother in the kitchen?" she

asked the woman, wishing with all her heart she didn't sound so needy. But now wasn't the time to worry about appearances, there was something far more important on her mind than the way she came across to Wendy's housekeeper.

Since Wendy had several brothers, the housekeeper needed to know which one she was referring to. Given that it was the youngest Mr. Fortune who came to pick up Katie every day, she honed in on him.

"Are you asking about Blake?" Juanita asked. "No, he has not come yet this morning." The housekeeper was accustomed to admitting Wendy's brother around eight-thirty every morning, when he came to pick Katie up to take her to Scott's house. "Perhaps he is running just a little late," she suggested.

"Or maybe he's just running," Katie said under her breath.

"Katie? Is that you standing out there in the hall?" Wendy called out as the housekeeper came in with her tray. "Come talk to me," she coaxed, beckoning for Katie to come into the room. She sounded even more restless than she had before she'd given birth. "The doctor said I needed to stay in bed for a few more days and if I go beyond the bathroom, Juanita tells on me," she said, nodding at the housekeeper.

Wendy was pretending to pout, but there was affection in her voice as she mentioned the older woman. About to say something else, Wendy's smile faded a little as she looked at Katie. Her friend appeared a bit disheveled as well as perturbed. Not to mentioned rather annoyed.

Wendy's antennae immediately went up. Something was definitely going on.

"My God, who died?" she asked, only half joking. When Katie didn't immediately answer, Wendy's eyes widened. "No one did, did they?" she asked nervously. She quickly reviewed a tally in her head. Her parents and family hadn't flown back yet, but as far as she knew, they were leaving this morning. Her husband was driving them all to San Antonio. "I just saw Marcos this morning before he left, but—"

"No *one* died," Katie assured her, putting emphasis on the second word.

"Okay," she replied cautiously. "But what did die?" Wendy wanted to know.

Katie stared off into space, waiting for the housekeeper to set down the tray and leave. When the woman finally did, closing the door behind her, Katie merely sighed. Silently, she called herself an idiot and seven kinds of a fool, but that didn't help anything or change anything, she thought darkly.

Blake was still racing into the arms of that woman. And she had helped to pave the way.

Oh, well, she tried to console herself, at least she'd had one good night out of it.

"Talk to me," Wendy urged and, from the sound of the exasperation in her voice, it wasn't the first time she'd said it. Katie hadn't even heard her say anything. "Didn't he take you out to dinner?" Wendy wanted to know.

"Yes, we had dinner," Katie replied. *And I volunteered to be dessert.*

"And?" Wendy pressed impatiently.

"He brought me home. Here," she clarified. in case Wendy thought she was referring to Scott's place, where Blake had been staying.

Nodding, she said again, "And?"

This time, the sigh was even deeper, coming from the very bottom of her soul. "And we made love."

Thrilled, Wendy clapped her hands together and all but cheered. "Wonderful!"

"Not so wonderful," Katie countered with a shake of her head.

Wendy's face fell as she obviously tried to fill in the blanks. "He's a bad lover?" There was an ocean of sympathy in her voice.

"Oh, no," Katie was quick to correct Wen-

dy's wrong impression. "He's an utterly magnificent lover with incredible stamina. We
made love twice and each time, he exceeded
anything I could have ever imagined." *And it's
going to be so wasted on Brittany*, she thought
with a huge pang of regret.

Wendy didn't understand. "If he was so
great, then why do you look like a kid who
just found out that not only is there no Santa
Claus, but she's going to be on the receiving
end of coal for the rest of her life?"

"Because Santa Claus is on his way to Atlanta this morning for his 'big' date with Brittany at the fund-raiser tomorrow," Katie bit off.
And that, he'd said more than once these past
few weeks, was going to be the beginning of
his life from here on in.

Wendy looked utterly horrified. "No, he's
not," she cried.

"Yes," Katie answered wearily, "he is." And
then, as much as it pained her, she gave Wendy
the information to back up what she was saying. "I do all of Blake's bookings for his trips.
I made this reservation for him and, since
he's not here this morning, having ducked
out sometime in the middle of the night," she
couldn't help adding bitterly, "it's safe to as-
sume that he is even now on his way to San
Antonio so that he can catch his flight to At-

lanta." Katie could feel angry tears forming in the corners of her eyes and she blinked hard to scatter them. "He's gone."

Wendy asked pointedly, "The real question here is, what are you going to do?"

Katie raised her eyes to Wendy's. "Do?" she echoed quizzically. *Do about what?*

"Yes. *Do*," she emphasized. "According to you, the two of you had a really great time last night. And then, apparently, my brother just took off early this morning without saying or writing a single word to you. That's just not like him," Wendy insisted, shaking her head. "God knows that man doesn't always connect the dots, but I've never known him to act like a Neanderthal jerk, either." Scooting to the edge of her bed, she gave Katie her theory. "My guess is that maybe being with you like that last night really shook him up. He saw you in a completely different light—"

"Yeah, he saw me naked," Katie said cynically.

"So, again," Wendy continued as if she hadn't been interrupted, "my question to you is, what are you going to do about it?"

Katie sank down on the bed, feeling frustrated, hurt and confused, not to mention angry. What made things particularly difficult was that she was feeling all these emotions at the same time.

Her shoulders rose and fell in an impotent shrug. "What can I do?"

"How about fighting for him?" Wendy challenged. The look in her eyes dared Katie to not just give up like this.

Having to "fight" for Blake was just another way of saying she was lowering herself, Katie thought. Lines had to be drawn somewhere.

"Look," she began patiently, "if Blake doesn't want me—"

Wendy cut her off. "I really doubt if that's the case." She saw the disbelief in Katie's eyes and she persisted. "More than likely, my brother's really scared."

"Scared," Katie repeated sarcastically. Her tone of voice told Wendy that she thought that was just a big crock.

But Wendy wasn't about to let Katie just cast that—and her chances of real happiness—aside. From where Wendy sat, it sounded like a very plausible explanation. Sometimes the thought of finding real love—committing to that love—was a scary proposition. Besides, she knew a thing or two about how the male mind worked. Katie had been the girl next door, but she hadn't actually grown up with three brothers the way Wendy had. That kind of hands-on experience inevitably taught a person things.

"Yes, scared," Wendy insisted as she emphasized the word. "My brother's been telling himself all this time that he's in love with Brittany, and then the lid blew off his world when he saw you last night all decked out and sexy." Wendy warmed up to her subject. "And, just like that, the two of you wind up making love. A guy who's in love with one woman doesn't make love to another woman with wild abandonment," she concluded knowingly.

Rather than challenge Wendy's choice of words—the woman had seen *too* many romantic comedies, she merely stated, "It happens all the time."

Wendy remained firm. "Not to Blake. He's the faithful type. Go after your man, Katie," she urged her best friend. "Make him realize that he wants *you, belongs* with you. Face it, Katie, if you go after him, what have you got to lose?"

"My dignity comes to mind," Katie answered tersely.

Wendy shook her head, dismissing the excuse. "Seems to me that dignity would provide you with cold comfort if you're all by yourself, thinking about what might have been if you'd only had the courage to act...." She let her voice trail off, watching to see Katie's re-action. She knew that Katie hated the thought of coming off like a coward.

And she was right.

"Okay," Katie finally cried, exasperated. "I'll go! But if this winds up blowing up in my face, I am going to come back and haunt you every day for the rest of my natural life—and then I'll come back as a ghost and continue to haunt you for all eternity."

Wendy smiled at her serenely. "I'm not wor-ried. Now, go, get a flight out," she said, shoo-ing her away with her hands as if Katie were a sparrow feeding on birdseed on the window-sill. "I'll have Juanita drive you to the airport when you're ready. Stop my brother from making a really stupid mistake." She leaned forward and took hold of Katie's hand. She squeezed it affectionately. "You're the best thing that ever happened to him and it's about time he admitted it and stopped running."

Katie *really* had her doubts about Wendy's take on the situation. But she knew that she re-ally *wished* that her friend was right.

"Whatever you say," Katie answered as she extricated herself and then walked out of the room.

She was walking faster by the time she reached her own bedroom.

* * *

As it turned out, because of a severe storm and the threat of a possible tornado in the Atlanta area, Katie couldn't get a flight out until the middle of the next day. By then, after spending the night at the airport, she'd had enough time to work herself up to the point that she was very close to having steam coming out of her ears.

The upshot of it was that she was no longer hurt, she was just plain angry. Angry at Blake for leaving her the way he had, without a word, as if she was some woman he'd encountered at a party and gone on to have casual sex with. There was definitely *nothing* casual about the sex they'd had—because, from her perspective, it hadn't been sex, it had been lovemaking.

She wouldn't have felt what she had, the earth wouldn't have moved the way it had, if she hadn't invested her emotions in it. And, she was certain, though he hadn't said a word, that Blake had felt the same way. They had even made love one more time in the middle of the night. She woken up to his stroking her arm. When she'd turned her head and seen the look in his eyes—not a look a man had when he'd had just casual sex with a person he didn't intend to see again—she'd been so moved that, well, one thing had led to another and then another and they'd made love again.

If he loved Brittany the way he claimed, that wouldn't have happened, she silently insisted as she sat rigidly in her seat, waiting for the Atlanta-bound plane to land so that she could get this speech off her chest and onto her lips.

Then, after he heard her out, if he still wanted to remain with Brittany, well, there wasn't anything she could do about that. If he was that mentally impaired, then he and Brittany deserved each other and she didn't want him anyway.

But even if that *did* come to pass, at least she would have gotten a chance to tell him what she thought of him for being so thoughtlessly self-centered—and for throwing away something precious and real that they could have had between them.

Not that she would have allowed Blake to get away with that, Katie thought as she braced herself for a landing. She would have confronted him as he tried to make his exit. She would have put him on the spot, even though she really wouldn't have known what to say.

At least this way, she told herself, she'd had time to get her thoughts in order. She only hoped that once she saw him, she wouldn't become so angry all over again that she just wound up sputtering at him like some old engine that had run out of gas.

Oh, God, was she fooling herself about him? Or was Wendy right? Had Blake beaten a hasty retreat in the middle of the night because what had happened between them had scared him?

If that was true, God knew he wasn't the only one. The intensity of what had gone on between them that night had scared her, too.

But what scared her even more was the thought of living the rest of her life *without* him.

With all her heart, she prayed that it was really the same way for him.

Chapter 15

This was a mistake.

He'd made a huge mistake, Blake thought, not for the first time in the past two days.

The uneasy thought that he was running *from* something rather than *to* something had hit him a couple of minutes before he'd presented his boarding pass to the attendant at the airport. Because it was around that time that it had finally hit him that the scenarios he was replaying in his head were all about the night he'd spent with Katie, and *not* the possible future he was going toward by flying back to Atlanta.

By flying back to Brittany.

It was Katie's face he saw when he closed

his eyes, Katie's skin he felt beneath his fingertips when he had allowed his mind to drift off for a moment as he'd stared out the window at the cloud formations on the horizon.

Yes, his pulse raced when he thought of Brittany, raced like the pulse of an adolescent involved with his first crush.

But the emotions that filled him when his thoughts turned to Katie belonged not to a boy, or to a hormonal teenager, but to a man, with a man's desires. And a man's needs.

Was it just a case of not knowing what he wanted? he'd challenged himself. Was he doomed just to want what he didn't have, or *couldn't* have at the moment?

Here he was, sitting at a table with Brittany at the fund-raiser, just as he had been fantasizing about for the past three weeks, and the only thing he could think about was Katie.

Would he be sitting and pining after Brittany if he were sitting here with Katie?

No, he realized, he wouldn't.

Because he hadn't.

When he had been with Katie that night, made love with Katie that night, there wasn't so much as a single molecule in his body that longed for Brittany. He'd wanted to be just where he was—with Katie. Making love with Katie.

And he'd known it, he told himself. Known it because, even as he landed in Atlanta, he'd called his father to let him know that he'd decided not to attend the fund-raiser.

His father had *not* been happy.

"You will attend." No request, just a command. The way it had always been. "You're representing the family at the fund-raiser. If you don't attend with Brittany, there'll be all sorts of talk about it by morning. I won't have it."

He'd wanted to say he didn't care. That people would always gossip because they had no lives of their own to occupy themselves with, but Blake knew how much his father despised gossips and rumors, wanting to always be above both. The man worked hard and he was exceedingly image-conscious.

"It's not like I'm asking you to marry her," his father went on to say. "Although—" he paused to speculate "—a merger between the two families might not be such a bad idea."

This was where Blake had drawn a line. He'd had to. "My marriage isn't going to be a merger, Dad," he'd said in no uncertain terms.

"Suit yourself," his father had responded, controlling his annoyance. "But you *are* attending the fund-raiser."

To refuse would have been to fuel a huge argument he'd wanted no part of, so Blake had agreed.

Which was how he came to be sitting here, at the fund-raiser, with a woman who was garnering all sorts of appreciative looks from men who obviously envied him his close proximity to her. He knew that a good many of those men would have given their eyeteeth to be in his position. As ever, Brittany was enchantingly beautiful—and he had absolutely nothing to say to her. Not a single word.

He had outgrown the Brittany he remembered. And, quite honestly, she was coming up lacking in every way when he compared her to Katie. She didn't have the deep commitments that Katie had—to her this fund-raiser wasn't so much about collecting money for the proposed new pediatric wing that the hospital wanted to build as it was about being seen—and admired—by the right people. She certainly didn't have the broad spectrum of interests that Katie had. Her interests all seemed to center around fashions—specifically, which ones were the most becoming on her.

She'd been expounding on the subject for what felt like an eternity now.

What could he have been thinking, wanting to win this woman? he upbraided himself. It would be like winning a gag gift, he thought, shaking his head.

Feeling trapped and counting the minutes until he could leave, Blake nodded his head periodically as Brittany droned on. Absently, he looked around the ballroom, searching for a familiar face that could afford him at least a temporary excuse to leave the table for a few minutes of respite. He really needed to clear his head of Brittany's endless chatter.

As he scanned the area, his eyes washed over a sea of faces, some very vaguely familiar, but most not.

Blake froze as his eyes widened.

Oh, God, now his mind was playing tricks on him. He actually thought that he saw Katie in the room. But that was impossible. This was a black tie, invitation only affair. She wouldn't have been able to get in.

Damn it, that *was* Katie, he realized. He'd know that determined expression on her face anywhere. It was hers exclusively. He stopped wondering *how* she'd gotten in and began wondering *why* she'd gotten in.

Was something wrong?

He sat up at attention as he watched her cut across the floor. She was heading for his table like a bullet—and right behind her, huffing and puffing as he attempted to catch up, was the heavyset man who had been standing at the entrance to the reserved ballroom, checking everyone's invitation.

Darting around the corpulent man as he tried once again—unsuccessfully—to grab her, Katie arrived at his and Brittany's table.

"So you *are* here," she declared angrily. A part of her had prayed that she wouldn't find him here. That at the last moment, he had realized how vapid Brittany was and had bowed out of the fund-raiser, sending in a silent pledge in his place.

So much for the power of prayer, Katie thought cynically.

Still huffing, the gatekeeper began apologizing. "I'm so sorry, Mr. Fortune—"

Blake waved away the man's words. "That's all right, she's my assistant."

The man slanted an annoyed look at Katie. "Well, as long as you know her..." the chagrinned gatekeeper murmured. Bowing, he was grateful to just disappear and put this behind him.

Blake's attention was already focused on Katie. "What are you do—?"

Blake got no further than that. Katie swung around and gave it to him with both barrels. She was going to say her piece if they were the last words she ever uttered.

"You have one hell of a nerve, you know that?" Out of the corner of her eye, she could see that people were looking their way. She didn't care. He had this coming to him. "Standing there and acting as if you're happy to see me when the dust is still settling from the way you rushed away from Wendy's house in the middle of the night. You didn't even have the decency to wait until I was up and look me in the eye!"

Everything she was saying was true. He knew that if he couldn't make her understand, he was going to lose her. "Katie, I—"

Brittany rose to her feet, all but knocking over her chair. "*This* is Katie?" Brittany cried in disbelief. Critical eyes looked Katie up and down as if she were nothing more than a mannequin in a boutique. "*This* is why you've been acting like a damn fool to me all evening?" she demanded incredulously.

"I thought you were ready to get serious, instead, you've been preoccupied all night. You haven't paid attention to a word I've said. My *brother* pays more attention to me than you did tonight. And now I understand why—well, I don't understand," Brittany corrected haughtily, a contemptuous look on her face as she regarded Katie, "but I see why." Tossing her hair over her shoulder, she planted impatient hands on her small hips. "Why didn't you just come out and *tell* me you were in love with someone else, instead of making me endure this evening?"

Katie's mouth dropped open and she stared at Blake as if she'd never seen him before. *Unbelievable!*

"You're in love with someone else besides Brittany?" she cried. How could she have *ever* been in love with this man? "What are you trying to do, start a harem? You think just because your last name is Fortune you can just go around, collecting whatever woman catches your fancy? Who the *hell* do you think you are?"

Bombarded from all sides by her rhetoric, Blake didn't know where to begin, but he knew he had to start somewhere. "No, I—"

Again, she wouldn't allow him to get further. Jabbing her forefinger in his chest, Katie continued to blast him.

"You know what's wrong with you? You don't know what you want. Love isn't something you can form a stupid campaign around. You don't execute 'strategies' to win someone, you watch them, you find out what they like, what makes them smile, and then you try your damnedest to do the things that *make* them smile. You protect love, you nurture love, you don't run a *campaign* for it."

She closed her eyes, willing herself not to cry, even though she could feel the angry tears starting to form. "You're obtuse and blind and it's my damn bad misfortune—pardon the pun— to be in love with you."

He focused in on the only thing that was important to him. "You're in—?"

"Yes!" she snapped. He might as well know. This way, maybe someday he'd realize just what it was that he had allowed to slip away. "Love. L-O-V-E. Love. I'm in love with you. Or was," she deliberately amended. What she felt for Blake wasn't in the past tense, but she was determined to get it to be. There was no point in loving a man who spread himself so thin and couldn't even recognize what had been right in front of him all along. "But I'm over you now. Oh, and by the way, I quit!" she shouted at Blake.

He stared at her, stunned, trying to pull everything together into a large, coherent whole. "But you can't quit now—"

Her eyes narrowed. "Oh, no? Just watch me!"

With that, Katie quickly spun on her heel and ran from the ballroom as fast as Cinderella had when she heard the clock in the tower chiming midnight.

It took him half a second to come to. When

he did, Blake rounded the table and took off after her.

Behind him, he heard Brittany call his name, demanding that he come back. He didn't bother turning around. He had no doubts that Brittany would find someone else to squire her around before the hour was up.

As for him, he had to make Katie listen to reason.

For a woman in high heels, he thought, Katie could really move. Determined to catch her before she got to the parking lot, he poured it on and finally managed to get within reaching distance of her, just outside the main ballroom.

Grabbing her arm, Blake spun her around to face him. Then, before she could begin to upbraid him all over again, he kissed her.

Long and hard.

Both breathless to begin with, they only became more so as the seconds ticked away and the kiss deepened in width and breadth.

When his lips finally left hers, Katie was dazed, lost in the heat and the passion of the moment. Wishing with all her heart that things could be just that simple. But then, as the last few minutes and what she'd heard from Brittany came flooding back to her, her indignation spiked. Her automatic reaction was to haul off and slap him across the face. Her fingers stung, but it was a small price to pay.

And then, in case he didn't already know why she'd hit him, Katie *told* him.

"That's for kissing me when you're in love with someone else," she shouted, struggling in vain to get out of his grasp.

Blake continued holding on to her, his grip tightening. He was determined to make her listen to him. She had to know the truth.

"The only person I'm in love with is you," he shouted back at her.

Because they were attracting attention again and she didn't want to be the object of anyone's pity, Katie forced herself to lower her voice.

"What about the other woman you've been seeing?" she accused.

"There *is* no other woman," Blake insisted. "Think," he implored when her face remained impassive. "The only woman I've been seeing night and day for the past few weeks is you. And you're wrong about my not knowing what I want. I *do* know what I want," he told her, his eyes caressing the soft, inviting contours of her face. "And it's you," he concluded in a whisper.

Right, like she really believed that. Just how gullible did he think she was?

"You want me," she said sarcastically. "And that's why you ran off yesterday morning and that's why you're here now, worshipping at Brittany's feet."

Okay, there he had her, Blake thought, beginning his rebuttal here. "Did Brittany *sound* as if she thought I was worshipping her?" he wanted to know. They both knew that the woman looked as if she'd wanted his head—or perhaps some other viable part of his body—on the chopping block.

"Well, no," Katie was forced to admit.

He looked at her for a long moment, debating the next thing he had to say. But, if he was going to get her back, he knew there *was* no debate. He was going to have to sacrifice his pride. There was no other way.

"And as for your first point," he began after taking a long breath, "much as it pains me to say this, I left you before you woke up because I felt all turned around. Everything I thought I wanted, I didn't anymore. And what I didn't think I wanted, I did."

He was trying to confuse her, she thought. "I don't understand."

Blake laughed shortly. That was exactly how he'd felt when he'd found himself unable to fight the strong attraction he'd felt for her the other evening. And even more so that night, after they'd made love and she lay sleeping in his arms.

"Welcome to the club. I needed to sort things out. To decide what I did want and what I didn't. By the time I got to Atlanta, I knew what I didn't want. I didn't want to reconnect with Brittany."

Oh, God, if she could only believe him. But the evidence all pointed otherwise. "And yet," she pointed out, "here you are."

"I'm here because you might have noticed that my father is very big on obligations and I'm the one who's supposed to be representing the family at this particular affair." Never mind that he'd initially lobbied for it. Once it was agreed upon, there was no getting out of it, short of a funeral. His.

"Since I was supposed to be Brittany's escort," he continued, "I went through with the charade, but that was all it was, a charade," Blake insisted. "I sat there, counting the minutes until I could leave. And then you came and sprang me," he concluded with a smile.

Her resistance was beginning to break down and she was starting to believe him. Maybe because she wanted to so badly.

"And caused a scene."

He shrugged indifferently. "It'll give them something to talk about," he said, referring to the people attending the fund-raiser.

But these were people he knew, people he

interacted with socially. Now that she was regaining her composure, she didn't want him feeling awkward around these people. "Do you care?" she wanted to know.

"The only thing I care about is hearing your answer when I show you this—" he took out a black velvet ring box from his pocket "—and ask you a question." He took a breath. *Here goes everything*, he thought. "Will you marry me?"

She couldn't help it, she'd been hurt so much, that naturally her suspicions were aroused again. "If you don't want to have anything to do with Brittany, what are you doing with an engagement ring in your pocket?" she asked.

"It *isn't* for her," he replied, his eyes on Katie's. "I was bringing the ring back to give to you." He held it out to her a second time. "It belonged to my great-great-grandmother. Family legend has it that she was a spitfire, too," he told her with a grin, then grew serious when she didn't immediately accept the ring. "We can reset it if you like."

"Don't you dare. It's beautiful just as it is." She looked at him for a long moment, as if trying to decide whether or not this was ultimately a joke. "You're serious?"

"Never more serious in my life," he swore. "I'm sorry I was too thickheaded to see what was right in front of me. I know I didn't deserve to have you sticking by me the way you did, especially when I came up with that harebrained scheme."

He couldn't even bring himself to say the name. What the hell had he been thinking, expecting her to help him win over Brittany? Another woman would have pushed him off a cliff—and he would have deserved it.

"You mean Project Brittany?" Katie asked innocently.

Blake winced. The mere sound of that was painful to him now. "The only project I want to undertake from here on in is to make you happy for the rest of your life."

Katie struck a poker face. "I haven't said yes yet," she pointed out.

He was all too aware of that. "I know and I don't blame you if you don't, but—"

With a sigh, she rolled her eyes and then placed her fingertips to his lips to still them. "Will you *please* stop talking? That's what's wrong with you marketing geniuses, you never stop talking," she marveled. Removing her fingertips, she immediately replaced them with her lips and kissed him—even longer and harder than he had kissed her.

"Does that mean yes?" he whispered against

her lips, wanting to hear her say the single, magical word.

Her eyes danced as she asked, "What do you think?"

Katie could have sworn that she tasted his smile as he lowered his mouth back to hers.

* * * * *

Get 4 FREE REWARDS!

We'll send you 2 FREE Books
plus 2 FREE Mystery Gifts.

Harlequin® Heartwarming™ Larger-Print books feature traditional values of home, family, community and—most of all—love.

FREE
Value Over
$20
